THE SMASHER

The
Smasher

Talmage Powell

PROLOGUE BOOKS

F+W Media, Inc.

Published in electronic format by
PROLOGUE BOOKS
an imprint of F+W Media, Inc.
10151 Carver Road
Blue Ash, Ohio 45242
www.prologuebooks.com

eISBN 10: 1-4405-3690-2
eISBN 13: 978-1-4405-3690-8
POD ISBN 10: 1-4405-5601-6
POD ISBN 13: 978-1-4405-5601-2

This work has been previously published in print format by:
The Macmillan Company, New York

TO MIMI

1

At the tail end of the day I went up to my hotel room. It was like a thousand other hotel rooms, each as barren as all the others no matter how fine the furnishings. It shared with all the others an aloofness, a loneliness, a feeling of being unoccupied even if someone were living in it.

I propped my brief case against the leg of the kneehole desk and dropped my hat and coat across the bed. I thought briefly of home; and then I sat down at the desk, opened the brief case, and got to work on the report.

It was a lengthy report and I lost track of time while I was working on it. Finished at last, I paused to light a cigarette. My eyes were gritty, my neck and back dull with fatigue.

As I leaned back in my chair, I happened to catch a glimpse of myself in the bureau mirror. I was just moody enough to study the mirrored face for a moment. I hadn't really looked at myself in a very long time. Women know what they look like. Few men do. We shave—and see the whiskers. Few of us know honestly what we look like.

The tiredness in the face gave me a faint jolt. It wasn't a face with greatness reflected in it, nor was it an evil face. The face of Mr. Everyman, who was five feet eleven, weight one-seventy. If there was deep tiredness in the face, there were also an open honesty and decency in the strength of jaw, chin, and forehead. A lock of black hair had fallen out of place and the gray eyes were squinted. The face was brushed with the day-end, black beard stubble.

I yawned, stretched, then turned my attention to the report again. I signed it: Steve Griffin.

I stood up, arching my back against the kink in it, and discovered that I was hungry.

It had grown dark outside while I'd worked, and with the darkness had come a fine rain, wet bits of anger against the windowpane.

I decided a shower would make for a more enjoyable dinner. While I got a fresh shirt from the bureau, I thought of Maureen and Penny and home. The three were components of a single unit in my mind. A wife, a fine little daughter, a comfortable living—I figured the loneliness and fatigue of the road work were worth while.

I was hungry for Maureen, for the warmth of her flesh and the passion I could stir in her.

And then the jangling of the telephone cut my thoughts short. I sighed, pitched my clean shirt on the bed, and walked to the small phone table at the head of the bed.

"Hello," I said. "Steve Griffin speaking."

"Long distance calling," the operator said. "Just a moment, please."

There was a pause. The operator said, "Go ahead, please."

And Maureen's voice came to me faintly, like the voice of a child lost in a long, dark tunnel. "Steve—I'm glad I caught you in!"

"Maureen!" I said. "This *is* a surprise. Wait a second. The connection seems bad. I'll tell the operator . . ."

"The connection's all right," she said in a stronger voice.

2

I gripped the phone. "Are you ill?"

"No, I . . ."

"Then it's Penny!"

"Penny's all right. She's watching some kid TV show."

I relaxed. "The sound of your voice had me worried for a second."

"Steve," she faltered, "it isn't a pleasure call."

I sat down slowly on the edge of the bed. "If both you and Penny are okay, then it must be some other kind of trouble."

"Yes, Steve. I want you to come home. Right away."

"Tonight?"

"Leave this minute! Please, Steve!" Her voice moved up the scale. Then she said quietly, simply, "A man's trying to kill me, Steve."

She was not a woman given to hysterics or wild imaginings. There was a chilling, my-back's-to-the-wall seriousness in her tone.

I sat a moment in shock.

"Did you hear me, Steve?"

"Of course," I said. "I'll leave here immediately."

"Thank you, darling," she sobbed. "He made the second attempt today. The first time might have been an accident. But not twice."

Twice. Twice someone had tried to kill my wife while I'd been going about my business knowing nothing of it.

There wasn't a reason in the world for anyone to want to do something like that.

"Are you certain, Maureen?" I asked, knowing that she wouldn't have called me without being certain.

"Yes, Steve," she said, her voice beginning to crack. "He's trying to run me down. With a car. He's trying to smash the life out of me, Steve!"

"Easy," I said.

"He tried the first time two days ago. I'd been out to the

plant nursery to get some shrubs for Dudley to set. The car came swinging into the intersection, tires screaming. He'd been waiting for me—in a heavy green sedan."

We had a heavy green sedan.

"A car exactly like ours," she said. "I jumped aside, and he missed me. It shook me—but I didn't think it was deliberate until today, Steve, when he had his second go at me. I went to the supermarket. I parked on the street instead of using the parking lot because the lot was jammed and hard to get into and out of. When I stepped from the curb, he came from nowhere. The same car. Heavy green sedan, turned into a monstrous weapon. . . ." Her words ended in a choked sound.

"My God, Maureen! Why?"

"Why?" she said. And she began crying. It wasn't like her. Maureen never cried, except over a homeless kitten or a sentimental story. It hit me suddenly that she wasn't crying because somebody was trying to kill her. She hadn't started crying until I'd asked that simple question, probed for the reason.

"I should have told you everything days ago, Steve," she said. "I wanted to. I've resolved to tell you, countless times—but when the moment came I never could get the words out. I haven't been very brave, Steve. I thought that time would swallow up the whole thing and I could get by without hurting you and Penny. And when you start hiding a thing, it gets harder and harder to drag it out into the light."

"Maureen—nothing could hurt me so much as having you in serious danger."

"Thank God for you, Steve! I'm ready to go to the police. But I want you here. I need you with me when I tell them."

"Tell them what, Maureen?"

"That I . . ."

"Yes, Maureen?"

4

"When you get home," she said very softly. "Hurry, darling!" The line went dead.

A hundred miles of blackness and rain. I was driving a coupe that belonged to the sales department. It was light, but I pushed it to the limit, skidding on the curves and chancing speed traps in the small towns I whipped through.

The night held an unreal quality. As unreal as our first meeting. That had happened in Korea, in the first weeks of the police action. Holding a commission in the reserves, I'd been recalled and shipped out when the Commies rolled over the 38th parallel.

Maureen was with a USO troupe, and when the Commie plane came over, a propeller-driven fighter of World War II vintage, Maureen and I had landed in the same ditch.

It was a muddy ditch, but as the strafing guns burped closer, I slammed her down and threw myself across her. Some wicked chunks of steel were sailing around in the air for a while, and a siren was wailing.

Maureen was far from relaxed, but she wasn't trembling, either. "Pardon me," she squeezed out, "but you've got your elbow in my mouth."

"Sorry," I said, and shifted my arms a little as the sound of the plane became a high-pitched scream.

I could hear his guns. I could sense the lacy pattern his bullets were making on the ground. I felt their hot fire stitching across my back.

It was over in seconds. The plane went away and activity returned to the ground. There was a lot of confusion. A strafing was the last thing expected in the area, and the job in Korea was still so new that a lot of people hadn't learned that the only predictable thing about a Commie is his unpredictability.

"Hey, soldier," Maureen tapped my shoulder, "he's gone."

I looked at her, a dumb grin on my face. I was grayed-out from shock.

"Get off me, you big lummox!" she said. She wriggled free of me, outraged, disgusted, and then she saw my back.

"Blood," she said, and went green.

She bounced out of the ditch and came back with two guys who had a stretcher between them. They lifted me out of the ditch. She ran alongside as we jogged toward the ambulance.

She looked small and breathless, and the breeze feathered her short, curly blond hair.

"I'll come to the hospital to see you, soldier," she said as they slid me into the ambulance.

"Swell," I said, speaking through my teeth because the numbness was going away.

She was bowed and penitent as she took a last look at me before they closed the ambulance door. The attendants were going around the ambulance to get into the seat. Then I saw her face framed in the rear window. Her eyes were wide. "What's your name?" she yelled.

The motor of the ambulance started. "Steve Griffin," I said. I wondered if she'd got it over the surge of the motor.

She'd got it. She was at the hospital when I came out of surgery, and every day afterward as long as she was in the area. Later, I tried to remember what we'd talked about. I couldn't. But I could remember that we were both eager to talk, interrupting and laughing.

I promised to look her up if I ever got back stateside.

My wounds were not serious in themselves. They healed quickly. But the aftermath was a muscle a bit too tight here, another slightly loose there. I felt fine and looked the same as ever, but the doctors said I'd never do any pick-and-shovel work.

The Old Man read me out of the service with a crack

about needing weaker minds and stronger backs. Then he forgot his rank, shook hands, and I was booked for passage home. I'd had my war—without ever coming face to face with a Commie.

I kept my promise to look Maureen up when I got back. We were both unattached. We went around together for a while. It wasn't a violent courtship. We were good company and enjoyed being together. We didn't have to do a lot, or chase to a flock of expensive places, to have a good time.

We were lonely. The things we'd seen overseas had changed us. We needed something. We decided it was each other.

One night we went to a party, and when it was over neither of us wanted to go home. We drove the rest of the night, crossed a state line, and got married early the next morning.

We rented a suite in a good hotel, had breakfast sent up, and later, when I held her in my arms, her eyes were deep, her body yielding.

"Steve," she whispered, "there's one more vow I'd like us to make."

"What is it?" I said.

"To work at making our marriage a success. So many people go into it nowadays expecting some kind of magic, expecting it to work automatically. A good marriage is something that has to be built."

"You're old-fashioned," I said.

"I only want to be married once, Steve."

She was at once femininely helpless and strong, scared and brave. This was the tenderest moment I'd ever experienced.

"It will work," I said.

And it had. It was not the perfect marriage, but we tried. We were not, I suppose, in love in the strictly romantic sense; we enjoyed and liked and appreciated each other. We had companionship and understanding. We were willing to accept each other's minor imperfections without hurt or irritation simply because neither was judging the other by the yardstick of a romantic ideal.

Our daughter Penny—four years old, blond curly hair, angels and imps in her blue eyes—cemented the marriage.

If it sounds dull, I've given the wrong impression. We visited and partied among a sizable group of friends. Maureen was intelligent, and quick to laugh. Her minor failing was her hatred of details, which was reflected in her housekeeping. The house was never dirty, but always a little cluttered. I didn't mind; it was comfortable.

If Maureen had a major failing, it was her need for constant appreciation. She wasn't catty or flirtatious, but when she entered a room she had to know that others knew she was there. The actress in her? Maybe. I was inclined to think the trait came from a sense of insecurity, never visible but never far from her.

The first lights of the city flashed by the coupe: drive-in theaters and restaurants, street lights making yellow halos in the rain.

I kept my foot heavy on the accelerator, threading my way through traffic. I hit the downtown red-light changes with luck. Office buildings and dark stores dropped behind. Streets began to be lined with trees, houses nestled in back of the shelter of lawns and hedges. I swung into the residential section where we lived—Meade Park—and my fingers were gripping the wheel so hard they ached.

It was midnight, and the rain was heavier than when I'd begun to drive. White, snug houses, some showing lights, flashed by.

I turned the corner onto our street, Tarrant Boulevard. Our house was halfway down the block. The living room was lighted and our car was parked under the carport.

I let out a long breath of relief.

8

2

I pulled the coupe in behind our heavy green sedan and sank back in the seat. I had such a cramp in my back muscles that getting out of the car was going to be an effort, but mostly I just wanted to sit there and look at the car and the lights and snugness of the house.

I got out of the coupe and put my hands against my kidneys to relax my back after the strain of the drive. I turned up my trench-coat collar and ducked across the lawn to the front door of the house.

I opened and closed the door, expecting Maureen to rush to me.

The living room was empty.

"Maureen?"

I waited until the house had swallowed the last echoes of the word.

Still in hat and coat, I gave the downstairs a quick search.

The silence of the house began to live.

I paused at the foot of the stairs, the emptiness and deserted aching of the house closing in about me.

After that phone call she would have been watching for me. She wasn't in the house. I knew that, even before I started up the stairs.

I went up anyway, taking the stairs two at a time. I reached the door to our bedroom, opened it, reached for the wall switch. Light flooded the room, which was empty. I turned back into the hall, breathing hard. I went to the door of Penny's room. I touched the knob, but was too weak for a moment to turn it. Finally, the door swung open. The light in the hallway fanned into her bedroom, sweeping across the little yellow ducks in the wallpaper design, splashing across her bed.

I held to the door jamb. She was in bed, sound asleep, one arm flung over her giant panda doll. The dim light caused her to stir. Her child's face was clean and fine in the light. She sighed, and sank back into deep sleep.

With a backward step, I closed the door on Penny's sleeping form. My head felt tight and dizzy as I retraced my steps to the stairwell and down the stairs.

I kept telling myself the main thing to do was not to go to pieces, to think what to do. She might have stepped out for a few minutes.

To that, the rain whispered a laugh.

I lighted a cigarette, forcing myself to keep calm. As I dropped the paper match in the ash tray, I saw the cigarette butt that was there. I picked it up. The butt was still soft and moist; it hadn't been snubbed out long. There was no lipstick on it, so Maureen hadn't smoked the cigarette. A man might have. And I tried to keep from thinking of which man.

I found myself at the front door, wet darkness in my face. For a second it was difficult to keep from yelling her name. She might have got away from him. She might be somewhere out there.

I could see no sign of her.

My mind was frantic in its efforts to avoid the big answer. I wanted to think that anything else was true. She'd got away from him and gone to a neighbor's house. But the surrounding houses, those close by, were all dark.

I closed the front door. I was beginning to shake.

Her phone call kept repeating itself like a very real whisper in my ear. The call that couldn't have come from a person who couldn't have possibly been touched by anything so fantastic as this sort of disappearance.

I found myself doing something with my hands. I looked at them. I'd taken the handkerchief from my pocket and begun wiping my palms. Already the handkerchief was sodden. I jammed it in my hip pocket and turned toward the alcove off the lower hallway. I had the average man's reluctance to call the police, but I didn't know what else to do.

In the small alcove, I picked up the phone and dialed. A quiet, bored voice cut short the ringing at the far end. "Police station, Precinct Five."

"I want to report a missing person."

"I'll connect you with the bureau."

A pause. I managed to light another cigarette while I waited.

A click. "Missing persons. Decoster speaking."

"I want to report a missing person."

"I figured as much. Your name?"

"Steve Griffin."

"Address?"

"Six-four-two Tarrant Boulevard. Listen, it's my wife . . ."

Decoster sighed, as if this were an oft-repeated routine. "Her name?"

"Maureen. She . . ."

"What makes you think she's missing, Mr. Griffin?"

"She wouldn't go out tonight . . ."

"Lots of folks go out in such weather."

"But our car was here, the lights on in the house, and our little girl asleep upstairs when I got home."

"Now look, Mr. Griffin," he soothed. "She might have been called out by a friend, any number of things. We don't list them as missing until they've been gone twenty-four hours."

"She may be dead before then."

"How's that?"

"Two hours ago I was a hundred miles downstate. She phoned me. She said someone was trying to kill her and begged me to come home. When I arrived here, there was no sign of her."

"I'll be right over," Decoster said.

I paced the floor until he got there, about ten minutes later. I was watching for him. I saw the police cruiser splash to a stop before the house. From the open front door I saw a tall thin man get out of the car. His raincoat flapped about his legs as he came through the rain to the house.

When he entered the living room I saw that he had loose, tired pouches beneath his eyes, and a thin, sallow face. His eyes were out of keeping with the rest of him. They were gray and sharp. He took off his hat. He was balding.

"Mr. Griffin?"

"Yes."

"I'm Decoster."

"I'm glad you came."

He looked from me, around the living room, as if it could tell him the sort of people with whom he was dealing.

"Give it to me," he said.

"You got most of it over the phone. She's not a hysterical sort of woman. She wouldn't have imagined someone was after her."

"Who?"

"I don't know. She said she'd tell me when I got here."

"I see. Man or woman?"

"She said it was a man."

"Then she knew who it was?"

"I think she did. He tried to run her down twice with a car. A heavy green sedan. Like the car we own."

12

"That's odd. Got a picture of her?"

I picked up a picture of Maureen from a corner table. As Decoster took it, I watched him.

"Pixie," he said, "mischievous. Slanted eyes. Nice teeth. She won't be hard to recognize."

He moved to the front door, stood facing the night, and made a gesture with his hand. A second later the cruiser door slammed, and a young cop in uniform came up the walk.

"I think we've got a missing one, all right," Decoster said. "Get a description of her on the air right away. You've already got the name and address."

"Yes, sir," the young cop said. He turned and, carrying Maureen's picture, vanished in the direction of the cruiser.

As Decoster came from the doorway, I said, "If you'd blanket the area, you might catch him."

The pale brows moved up.

"When I came in," I explained, "I found a still moist cigarette butt in the ash tray. It was free of lipstick. My wife didn't smoke it, I'm sure. He must have."

Decoster looked at my face. "Sit down," he suggested, "and we'll talk."

"Talk! Why don't you do something?"

He touched my shoulder. "I understand your feelings— but don't take them out on us."

"Sorry," I said.

"That's all right," he remarked. "Even if you're correct in your guess about the cigarette, he won't be in the open, a sitting duck waiting with her for us. He could be in any part of the city by this time. It'll be the system that nails him, Griffin. A criminal may be smarter than an individual cop, half a dozen individual cops, but the system is the product of too many brains. It's been tried and tested and refined too many times. The system will get him. Now," he suggested, giving me his undivided attention as if I were the only customer he'd had in the past five years, "tell me about her."

I sat down slowly. "What do you want to know?"

"Anything you can think of. Her habits, friends, likes, dislikes, activities. Her enemies."

"She didn't have any—not that kind."

He smiled and waited, and I went cold all over. The message was in his eyes: Oh, yes, she did; she had at least one of that kind.

"I'll kill him," I said. "If he harms her, I'll kill him."

"You were going to tell me about her," Decoster said.

"Yes," I said. I sagged suddenly with fatigue, looking at the floor, trying to think of something to say about her. "She was a woman—like a million other women. She had her home and family. This was her world. Violence and deviltry were things that appeared only in newspaper headlines."

I found relief in talking of her. Decoster was a good listener, his attention unwavering.

I tried to show him what she was like, her strange mixture of maturity and perpetual adolescence. Just when you were convinced that her outlook would be forever youthful and unsullied, she would reveal a knowledge of life that should have belonged to an ancient philosopher. At the moment it seemed she would shy from a puppy's bark, she would show a flash of grit and determination sufficient to put a mastiff to flight.

With a nod, a word, a facial expression, Decoster kept me talking.

I told him how we'd met, how we lived. He learned that she'd been an actress who'd achieved only a very minor success. Her eyes still became nostalgic if talk turned to things theatrical.

"Perhaps she's still gnawed by ambition," Decoster said, careful to keep mention of her in the present tense.

"She was never 'gnawed by ambition,' as you put it. She

14

enjoyed acting. She liked late hours and the excitement of being in the center of the stage. But she's spoken very little of her acting since Penny was born."

"I see. What about yourself?"

"What do you mean?"

"How do you earn your living?"

"I'm a minor partner in a plastics firm headed by Willis Burke. We became friends in Japan, during the Korean action."

"He come from the Burke family the downtown street's named after?"

I nodded. "His family have been prominent here for several generations."

"I know. The history of this town has been spotted with the name Burke since the city was chartered."

"Will used an inheritance to put up most of the money when we started the firm," I said. "He's the executive, the organizer, the desk man. I run things in the field."

"Then you're away from home a great deal?"

"Most of the time. . . ." I stopped speaking. We sat looking at each other. Carefully, I put my hands on the arms of the chair. "Do all cops have dirty minds?"

"Now, you just remember this"—Decoster's face seemed longer, thinner: "There are only three possible explanations for someone being after her, Griffin. First, the man might be a nut. Second, he might have mistaken her for someone else."

"And third?"

"Third—in your absences she's been up to something that made somebody want to kill her."

He said it gently.

I held to the arms of the chair to keep from hitting him.

3

The door chimes sounded. I got out of my chair and reached the door before Decoster.

Willis Burke was outside, rain speckles on his bare head and dark suit.

"Oh—it's you," I said. "Hello, Will."

He waggled a finger at me. He smelled slightly alcoholic. "Saw the company car in the driveway as I passed by. Suppose now you'll want a bonus for finishing . . ."

"Come in, Will. Something's happened."

His brows knitted. He stepped into the living room, giving Decoster a look. Will was a tall man, but solid enough with muscle to give the appearance of stockiness. He glowed with health, and the drinks he'd had. He carried himself with the unconscious assurance that comes from never having to worry about money. At thirty-five his face was still that of the college senior who is president of the student body. A square face with a cleft chin. Heavy but even brows. Brown hair that formed a widow's peak on the high, clear forehead.

I closed the door. Will turned to me, sensing that my words carried more than a casual implication.

"This is Mr. Decoster, Will. A policeman."

16

"You in trouble, Steve? We'll fix everything up in jig time."

"Will, Maureen has disappeared."

Looking at him, I could see the words wipe the alcoholic haze from his brain. His eyes came to meet mine, soberly.

"I hope I didn't hear you correctly, Steve."

"I'm afraid you did."

"When?"

"Tonight."

"How could it be?" Will said, shock in his eyes. "For what possible reason?"

"That's what we'd like to know," Decoster said. "It would point to the man who took her."

"Took her?" Will said.

"He apparently came here tonight and forced her to go with him," I said, "only a short time before I arrived."

"My God," Will said simply. "I honestly need a drink, Steve."

"Over there in the dining area," I said. "Left side of the buffet."

Will stumbled through the archway between the living and dining rooms. He got a fifth of bourbon out of the buffet and poured himself a drink. Decoster watched him patiently.

In the shadowed dining room, Will threw the first drink down his throat, poured a second in his glass, and carried it back to the living room.

"I'm a little confused," he admitted. "I expected you to be a hundred miles away from here tonight, Steve. Instead, I find you here and Maureen gone."

"She phoned me. She begged me to come home. Somebody's been trying to kill her. He made two attempts. Tonight—well, tonight they've got a description of her on the air and we're hoping he's going to fumble the third time."

Will groped his way to a chair. "Lemme get this straight.

17

She called. Life threatened twice. Gone when you got here. Look —this is real, isn't it? I'm not passed out and dreaming?"

"You're sober enough," Decoster said.

Will looked up at the detective dumbly. "No wonder she's been looking as if sleep and she had become strangers."

"When did you last see her, Mr. Burke?" Decoster asked.

"Yesterday. In the evening. Carla, my wife, and I invited Maureen to dinner. We'd noticed how peaked Maureen was looking. Decided she needed an evening. But it didn't work out."

"No?"

Will shrugged. "Carla and I—we had words. We often do. Words over anything. I forget what the set-to last night started over—oh, yes, Carla had forgotten to make reservations at the Penguin Club."

"The three of you were going there?"

"We'd planned on it. But when dinner was over and we were ready to start out, Carla and I discovered neither of us had made reservations. It's pretty hard to get in there without them."

"Oh," Decoster said mildly, "even a portal so high on the social ladder should fall open to a Burke."

Will looked at him, his face undergoing a change of expression. He looked rugged and tough. And yet there was a faint boyish hurt deep in his eyes, hurt he had carried with him for many years. Will had always stood on his own two feet and made his own way. But no matter what he did, he never felt a complete man. He never fully escaped the reminder that he was a Burke, born to plush, with a gold spoon in his mouth.

Will's expression softened to a patient weariness. "Anyhow," he said, looking at his glass, "we didn't go to the club. Carla blamed everything on me. Said I should have called her during the day and reminded her that she'd promised to take care of the reservations. Said I knew what busy days she had, and how could she be expected to think of everything."

18

"Go on," Decoster prompted.

"Usually Maureen was amused at our tiffs. She would console Carla and cheer me along with a smile and a wink. Last night, however, she listened a few moments and told us both to shut up. How could we be so upset and irritated by minor things, she asked, when there was so much danger and death in the world. Then she walked right out on us. Carla was so flabbergasted she didn't think to criticize me once during the rest of the evening."

"That's the last time you heard from Mrs. Griffin?"

"She called me at the office today," Will replied. "Said she wanted to apologize for last night. Wasn't herself, she said. Bad migraine headache. I told her to think nothing more of it, except to be glad she'd done Carla and me a favor. Did us good, Carla and me, to see ourselves a little differently."

"That was the extent of the conversation?"

"Well, I said I'd noticed she hadn't been looking too well, and asked if I could give her an assist. She said no, it was something she'd have to take care of herself." Will glanced at me. "Steve's a hard worker, and I thought maybe Maureen was just plain tired out. I said she and Steve should take a vacation, go away for a couple of weeks, get away from it all. She said she'd think about it, and rang off." Will sighed. "If I'd known she was desperate, I wouldn't have let her stay here alone, of course."

"Did Mrs. Burke see Mrs. Griffin today?"

"I don't know. You can ask her. I haven't seen much of Carla myself."

"More words?"

Will nodded. "Last night and this morning I got the impression Carla, as well as myself, was ashamed of last night. The cure was short-lived. Carla was her own dear self when I went home tonight. After dinner I went out to have a few."

"I take it that the two families have a stronger link than the mere business relationship," Decoster said.

"We're friends," Will said. "Sometimes I come here when I want a quiet dinner." His glance moved about the living room, a comfortable servants' quarters compared to his place. "Cozy. Relaxing. Not like the joint where I hang my hat."

"How often do you come when Mr. Griffin isn't home?" Decoster asked mildly.

The cleft deepened in Will's chin. "Public servant, how would you like a punch in the nose?"

"You're not as sober as we thought," Decoster said. "Or else you're very foolish. Now answer my question, please."

Will measured the cop. Then he decided to talk instead of punch. "In the first place, I don't court scandal," he said. He glanced at me. "Second, Steve happens to be my friend. Third, any time I hanker after strange flesh I know the proper places to find it. Fourth, you just don't know the loyalty that's in Steve's wife, brother."

I was glad he'd said that and I was glad he'd said it in such a way. Decoster's insinuation about Maureen was gnawing at my mind, despite my efforts to ignore it.

"And yet, Mr. Burke," Decoster said in a very low voice, "Mrs. Griffin admitted to her husband that a man was trying to kill her."

Will reared to his feet. "So a man's trying to kill her! Does it prove she was what you're trying to make her out?"

"I'm investigating a case," Decoster snapped, "not arguing with an overgrown college kid."

Will was literally trembling. "Steve, I've got to get out of here. Call me when this character has gone."

"Take it easy," I said.

"You're not going anywhere, Mr. Burke," Decoster said. "You just get one thing straight. A woman has disappeared. It's up to me to find out why. I'm going to dig out the reason, no matter how much dirt I have to throw."

"You won't find any dirt to throw. Not about her," Will said. "And when this is over, I'm going to hear you apologize."

"I'll do that," Decoster said seriously, "if the natural chain of events should call for it."

The phone rang.

I left them standing, Will seething, Decoster like a gray, haggard old eagle whose lifetime has been spent in warfare.

I entered the alcove off the hallway and picked up the phone on its second ring.

"Steve Griffin."

"Precinct Five," a voice said. "Is Decoster there?"

"Yes." My hand was tight on the phone. "Have you—"

"Put Decoster on," the voice said.

I laid the phone down and called Decoster. I stood just inside the living room and watched as he crossed the hallway and picked up the phone.

Will drifted up beside me. I heard him saying words to the effect that everything would turn out all right, that we'd stand together, and that we mustn't let worry handicap us.

I didn't take my eyes off Decoster.

"This is Decoster," he said after he'd placed the phone carefully against his ear.

Then he said, "Oh."

Next he said, "I see."

An expression of anguish crossed his thin face. He closed his eyes for a moment.

Finally he said: "We'll need Elda Darrity over here. Send her at once."

He cradled the phone. He didn't look at me right away.

"You've got a lead on her—so quickly?" I said.

Decoster turned and faced me. "A woman answering your wife's description was just brought into the morgue."

"Why—" said Will. "Why—that can't be!"

A strange thing had happened to the house. Its walls seemed to have expanded with terrific speed, leaving me standing naked and alone in a cold, dark place.

Then Decoster's face swam back into focus. He was gripping my arm. "It may be a mistake. It might not be her. You'll have to go down and say for sure."

"Yes," I said. "I understand." I turned blindly into the living room. Then I stopped. "You said yourself she would be easy to recognize. How could it be a mistake?"

"Cops make them, same as anybody else," Decoster said.

Somewhere in the fog I heard Will's voice. "Get a grip on yourself, Steve. Don't even think it. It *has* to be a mistake."

I lifted my head. I was looking toward the ceiling, but I wasn't seeing it. I was thinking of her up there asleep. So young. So innocent. So unhurt.

"My little girl . . ." I said.

"I'm having a policewoman sent over," Decoster answered. "Sergeant Elda Darrity is young and kind. She likes kids."

"If Penny wakes up . . ."

"Sergeant Darrity will know what to do," Decoster assured me.

"Steve," Will said, "I'll go with you. I'll have Carla come over and stay with Penny."

"I'd like to have you go with me," I said. "But don't upset Carla." I preferred to have the policewoman in the house if Penny woke. Carla prattled. She might say too much, too soon, to a little girl.

"Sergeant Darrity will be rushed over by cruiser," Decoster said. "It will take her only a few minutes to get here. Meanwhile, why don't you get into your hat and coat?"

I glanced around. For a second I could remember nothing of the arrangement of the house. The furniture looked strange.

Then I saw my hat and coat on a chair where I'd dropped

22

them some time after I'd come in. I couldn't remember taking them off.

Obediently, I put on the hat and coat.

A little later, through the window, I saw a second police cruiser roll to a stop outside.

4

The policewoman was a pleasant and capable-looking brunette. She was husky, with kindness in her face. Decoster introduced us.

"You needn't worry about your little girl, Mr. Griffin," Elda Darrity said with a kind smile.

"Thanks," I said. "Sometimes if she happens to wake at night her mother makes her a small cup of hot chocolate. I'm sure there's cocoa and milk in the kitchen."

The policewoman nodded and, with Will and Decoster flanking me, I went out into the night.

The rain had slacked off, and little tendrils of fog rose from a manhole cover in the middle of the street. The night air was still very wet, the rain coming now like a heavy falling dew.

The three of us got into the back seat of the cruiser Decoster had arrived in. The young cop in uniform was at the wheel. He started the motor and the squad car pulled away.

I sat and watched the windshield wipers clear away the continual fall of mist. It was the first time in my life I'd ever ridden in a police cruiser. The passage of a squad car, or an ambulance, had always been an object of idle curiosity to me. In the future I'd know what it was like to be a passenger.

Decoster spoke little. Will sat as if trying to think of

something to say. The odor of bourbon permeated the closed cruiser.

Precinct Five station house was not far from where I lived. I watched the black, slick street roll up under us. The young cop didn't take the turn.

Of course not.

We were headed for the morgue.

I remembered how humbly and tenderly she had watched them put me into the ambulance. "I'll come to the hospital to see you, soldier. . . ."

We rolled down a deserted street in the older part of town. The cop braked the cruiser to a stop before an old brownstone building.

We got out of the car. Decoster first, I behind him, Will after me. We crossed the sidewalk and walked up wide stone steps. They were so old they had scooped-out places from the tread of countless feet.

Decoster pulled open one of the double frosted glass doors that shed a milky light over the steps.

"It's all a mistake," Will said to me quietly. "It couldn't be Maureen. In a minute you'll see that it's all a mistake, Steve."

I didn't say anything. Decoster was holding the door for me. I went inside.

We were in a high gloomy wide hallway. There was a cubicle to one side cut off from the hallway by a waist-high desk. Behind the desk a fleshy middle-aged man sat beside a switchboard. He was reading a magazine. He laid it aside, dog-earing a page to mark his place. His face was puffy and his eyes lacked luster. Keeper of the dead.

"Hello, Decoster."

"How are you, Rankin?"

Rankin shrugged. "You want to see that woman we brought in tonight?"

Decoster nodded.

"She's a mess," Rankin said in a low tone. "I guess it'll be tomorrow afternoon before the pathologist gets around to her for a P.M. You can go on back. I'll buzz Enloe. He's on duty."

"Okay," said Decoster.

I followed him down the hallway, a place of stark light and echoes. The rubber tile cried softly beneath our wet shoe soles, and the corners of the vaulted hall held the sounds for just an instant.

Halfway down the hall, Decoster turned to Will.

"You'd better wait here."

"All right," Will said. There was a slick sheen of sweat on his face. He seemed grateful to remain right where he was. There were some polished dark wooden benches along the wall. He went over and sat on one of them.

Decoster and I reached the double oak doors at the end of the hallway. Decoster knocked. There was the sound of a lock-trip buzzer, and Decoster opened the door.

The room might have been the ballroom of a mansion at one time. It was very large, with a domed ceiling. If ever there had been windows, they had been walled in. At the far end of the room was another set of wide double doors, the emergency entrance from outside.

Light for the room was supplied by two overhead fixtures. It was a bright light, but not hot. It was like a dazzling light reflected from ice.

Along the inner wall of the room was a bank of deep square lockers, each with its own door, lock, and tag. Temporary tombs. Somewhere deep in the heart of the building a motor pulsed as it fed refrigerant to the vaults. The motor was a little heart, beat, beat, beating. Beating to keep corruption from its dead.

A young man in a white smock came into the room from a

26

doorway to my left that I hadn't noticed before. He had a pleasant, craggy face and sandy hair. He was putting on rubber gloves.

"Hi, shamus," he said to Decoster.

"Hello, Enloe."

"You're Mr. Griffin?" Enloe said to me as he slipped a surgical mask over the lower portion of his face.

"Yes," I said.

"I hope they've called you down here for nothing," he said through the mask.

I nodded. My throat became too dry to speak.

Enloe moved down the row of lockers. He paused about two-thirds of the way down. He looked at the tag on the front of the locker, grasped the handle, and pulled. The slab was perfectly engineered. It slid outward at his touch, silent, in precise balance.

I felt the waft of cold that came from the locker. It enveloped me as I looked at the sheet-covered form on the slab.

Enloe turned back the sheet.

I looked once and stumbled away. I covered my face with my hands. I could hear my groans reaching out to the walls of the room, reaching to the ceiling.

After a little while I was able to stop.

There is no recalling a minute in time.

There was no way of bringing her back.

She was beyond all the mourning in the world.

Nothing was left inside me except the horror of knowing that she had lived in a world where such a thing could happen to her. And out of the horror came revulsion for the creature who had done it. And from that came hate.

"I'm sorry," Decoster said in the kindest tone he had used so far. "But are you positive?"

I looked at him.

27

"It's my duty to ask you," he said.

"I'm positive," I said. "That's Maureen. That's my wife."

"I'll take you home," he said.

"You've got to find out who he is," I said.

"We will. Only a small percentage ever get away with it."

"Don't let him be in that percentage, Decoster. Only find him. He'll get what's coming to him then. If a shyster lawyer sneaks him out of it, I'll be waiting."

Enloe had put the sheet back over her. I heard the faint whisper of the steel rollers as she was slid back into the dark little hole to become only a name on a tag.

Decoster kept his hand on my arm as we went back into the hallway. Will got up from the bench. He stood quite still, not coming forward, simply looking at my face. He aged ten years as he found his answer.

I fumbled a cigarette between my lips, and one of them held a light for me.

I tried to recall her laugh. I tried to remember the way she had moved, young, warm, and so alive. Skin firm and clear. Eyes dancing with merriment.

But she was a stranger beyond recall. All I could remember was the broken hulk on the cold slab, its clothing sodden and bloodstained, its hair wet and tangled about the small, triangular face.

Tomorrow Penny would wake and ask for her mother.

The squad car retraced its earlier path, through the swirl of street lights, down the long lanes of dark mist.

We stopped in front of the house. Will, Decoster, and I got out, moved up the walk, and went inside the house.

The policewoman was standing in the living room. She looked at Decoster, and he gave her a faint nod.

"I'm terribly sorry, Mr. Griffin," Elda Darrity said.

"Thank you," I said.

"Would you like to have me stay the rest of the night in case the little girl wakes up?"

"No, I can take care of everything. Thanks, anyway."

She reached forward impulsively and laid her hand on my arm. "I know it sounds empty, Mr. Griffin, but I'm sure everything will be all right someday."

But everything was all wrong now. Everything was out of kilter. Everything was warped, rotten, and unfair.

She was needed here. Penny needed her. I needed her.

Somewhere in the city was the man who had done this thing. Perhaps he was smiling to himself or pouring himself a drink. Perhaps he felt powerful and successful, smarter than all the rest of crawling humanity combined. Or perhaps he was grim with worry as his mind went over and over his crime, seeking flaws, searching for the smallest possible mistake.

"Sure you'll be okay?" Decoster asked.

I nodded.

"I'm going to stick around," Will told Decoster.

"Good," Decoster said. He turned to me again. "Relax if you can, Griffin, and get some rest. We'll need all the help we can get. You'll be talking to several people in the morning."

I nodded. Decoster and the policewoman went out.

I sat down on the living-room couch and put my face in my palms. I heard Will in the dining room getting whisky. He came back with the bottle in his hand. "A short one, Steve?"

I shook my head. I watched him pour a small drink. He looked tired, almost ill. He didn't toss off the drink in his usual fashion. He sat with his elbows on his knees, the glass held in both hands.

"Steve—I didn't exactly level with Decoster."

"What do you mean?"

"I've been here when you were away. Now that this terrible thing has happened, I must tell you. I have to make you understand. Steve, she was like a sister to me." His voice faded away.

I sat perfectly still. "Go on, Will."

He made a vague gesture with his hand. "I know this is risking one thing I treasure a lot, Steve—our friendship. But I won't take the risk of having you learn from someone else. It was all completely innocent, but it might look different if you hear about it in a roundabout way."

He stopped speaking again. He seemed to need help from me. I let him sweat. I didn't say anything.

"She wasn't the 100 per cent young poised matron you wanted her to be, Steve. God knows she tried. For your sake—and Penny's.

"She had qualities she felt she should get the better of. They weren't really bad. Impulsive generosity. A lonely need for applause, approbation. A too youthful streak in her that needed constant urging to be adult."

"I knew my wife, Will. I knew her qualities."

"I know you did. And she knew you, Steve. She admired your character, your strength and realistic outlook. She was a different person when you were near."

My eyes nailed him. "And what kind of person was she when I wasn't near?"

"I didn't say that, Steve. I didn't say she was different in that way."

"You implied it."

"No—I'm saying this badly."

"Can it be said well?"

His eyes were miserable. "I had that coming, maybe. She didn't."

"I wasn't saying it to her, Will. You were going to tell me—about you and her."

"I've told you, and I've told you why. I'm your friend. I was her friend. She was lonely sometimes. So was I."

30

"Was this loneliness a chronic disease when I was out of town?"

"No, Steve, and that's the God's truth! We were not alone often. Neither of us entertained any thought of an affair. We would talk and have dinner, maybe go for a ride and make jokes that only children would laugh at."

"Like you were still in college," I said.

He stared at the carpet and said nothing.

"Just a big, handsome college kid," I said. "Will, when are you going to grow up?"

"I grew up a long time ago, Steve," he said softly. "I came into the world grown up. This other—it's an act, long practiced, to forget once in a while that I'm grown up, a grown-up sonofabitch who's hated by a lot of people in this town because I was born lousy with money and with the name of Burke. Strangers dislike me sometimes for that reason alone. Like Decoster. I never saw him before tonight, but he had to get his dig in because I'm a Burke. Like waiters. Do you ever have a waiter snub you, Steve?"

"Not as a rule."

"And as a rule, I don't. But they do. They try. They do it with a secretive sneer. Either fawning all over me or snubbing me. I don't want either, Steve. I just want to be treated like a human being. Am I getting it across to you? I had to grow up fast, because I was never permitted to be just another human being. Maureen understood. Instinctively. With all the kindness and goodness that were in her. I never had to explain it. She just understood —and was my friend, simply and honestly, because she liked me."

He looked at me with suffering in his eyes. He didn't look like the Will I'd always seen. Maybe it was the lighting, or the angle of his face.

It came to me with a shock that Will was poor. He wasn't the rich man the world saw, nor the egotist. He wore the poise of generations of breeding, and, mostly, he did it well. Now I knew that even when he was wearing it well, he did so like a man making the best of a flimsy garment in chill weather. All his wealth couldn't buy the protection he needed.

"Does Carla know?" I asked.

"I haven't told her. I don't think she'd understand my coming here. Steve, you want me to get out?"

"No," I said. "I think you've told me the truth. I think you lied to Decoster because in your way of looking at things you felt you were protecting my honor. You're very likely right about it, too. So I'm not asking you to leave, Will. But don't you think you'd better get back to Carla?"

"She'll be all right. I'll stay here. There might be something I can do. And thanks, Steve."

"You can sleep in the den."

"If I decide I want to turn in."

I went out of the living room, up the silent, hateful stairway. I closed the door of the master bedroom behind me.

I looked at the emptiness of the twin beds. I walked to her bed and sat down. I ran my hand gently over the clean, fresh linen. I sat that way for a little time; then I opened the drawer of her bedside table.

It was a catchall, cluttered, mussed. This room was like a part of her, orderly, warm; and this drawer was a little hidden portion of her, a tumbled, jumbled tangle of odds and ends.

I turned her rhinestone earrings in my palm. The drawer had captured them some evening when she'd come home tired and happy, thrown herself across the bed, and pulled the bits of jewelry from her ears.

I looked at a wrinkled piece of Kleenex that carried the bright red imprint of her lips.

I felt as if I would strangle.

I flipped through her checkbook, wondering how many checks she'd forgotten to stub.

32

There was a folder-bound manuscript of a play in the drawer. I flipped through the typewritten pages. I wondered if she had written it; then I saw that she hadn't. The author's name was on the first page. I'd missed it at first. I saw it as I was putting the play back in the drawer. Randy Price. The address was here in town.

I didn't recall having met a Randy Price. Maybe I had. At parties Maureen had always known far more people than I had. She would introduce them to me with such rapidity that often I couldn't remember who it was she was chattering about on the way home.

Maybe this Randy Price was a member of her little theater group and she'd decided to act in an amateur production. She would have planned it as a secret to be sprung on me at some moment her sharp intuition told her would afford the most surprise.

Thinking about it, I moved to the wall switch, turned off the light, and lay down on my own bed.

I felt the emptiness of the bed beside me. I didn't get to sleep for a long time.

5

The girl came to the house early the next morning. Will was asleep in the den, and Penny had not awakened yet. I was in the kitchen making coffee and thinking about one of the toughest problems I'd ever faced—how to tell Penny—when the door chimes sounded.

My first thought was the police.

They'd caught him.

His nerve had broken.

He'd walked in and given up.

He was a dead sonofabitch.

I jerked the door open, and the violence of my motion caused the girl to step back.

My shoulders dropped a little. "Sorry," I said. "I was expecting someone."

"You must be Steven," the girl said. "I'm Vicky Clayton."

She was a tall, attractive girl. Her face was well defined, with high cheekbones and a warm, full-lipped mouth. She had large, dark brown eyes and glossy brown hair which waved slightly and almost touched her shoulders. She was dressed in a quiet gray tailored suit. The warmth of her voice was one more detail adding up to sincerity and friendliness.

34

She saw the blankness in my face. "Maureen never mentioned me?" Beneath, she became a little nervous. It showed in the way she gripped the newspaper in her left hand.

"She might have, Miss Clayton. My mind isn't working too well this morning."

"Of course," she said. The touch of her hand on my wrist was a generous, impulsive gesture. "I'm sorry, Steven," she said simply. "Maureen and I were friends once."

"You know?"

"Yes."

I glanced at the rolled-up paper in her hand. "It's in there?" She nodded.

Of course. How could it fail to be? Life continued. Newspapers were published several times every day.

We were still standing in the doorway. I stepped aside. "Please come in."

She entered the living room.

"Would you like some coffee?" I asked.

She didn't protest or explain that it was an awkward time for her to be here. She said, "Thank you. I'd like some very much."

"I just finished making it."

We went in the dining room. The electric percolator in the kitchen had cut itself off. I walked to the kitchen and brought in the percolator, cups and saucers. Cream and sugar were already on the table.

We sat down and I poured coffee and put some bread in the toaster. Vicky Clayton's newspaper was on the dining table. I picked it up. The item was front page, but not in large headlines.

A woman had been run over by an automobile. She was a wife and mother; she had once been an actress. Police were searching for the death-dealing car.

I laid the paper down quickly.

The toaster clicked, and I took the browned slices of bread out.

"Have you lived here long, Miss Clayton?"

"I came here only a few days ago to visit relatives. I phoned Maureen."

"I guess I was out of town."

"Yes, she told me she'd married a man who traveled. For some concern that makes furniture?"

"Plastics."

"We were planning a lunch and old-times talk, Maureen and I."

"You knew her in show business?"

"Yes," Vicky Clayton said. "I was a terrible actress. Maureen used to try to help me."

"She was like that."

"She would use her spare time to coach me. I think she could have been a really great actress if she'd wanted to badly enough."

"She liked it. She wanted to."

"Oh, as a game. Wasn't she like that?"

"She was," I said.

"She wanted what she had here a lot more," Vicky said, glancing around the dining room, into the living room, then in the other direction to that portion of the white and chrome kitchen that was visible.

There was a sound of racing footsteps pattering overhead and down the stairs. In rumpled pajamas, Penny ran into the dining room. She stopped short, seeing me and the stranger. Then she ran forward and bounced into my lap. "Daddy! You're home!"

She scrambled down and, before I could stop her, scurried toward the kitchen.

"Mommy, daddy's home!"

Vicky Clayton paled and glanced away.

36

"Mommy . . ."

Penny saw that the kitchen was empty. She came back to me. I picked her up, swung her high.

"Is Mommy still asleep?" she asked.

"Penny," I said, setting her on the floor. Then I couldn't say anything else.

Vicky rose. "Hi, Penny. I'm Vicky. Your mother had to go away on a trip. And you know something? I forgot to ask her what you like for breakfast."

"Oatmeal," Penny said, "with lots of sugar on it."

"Fine," Vicky said. She held out her hand, and Penny, always too exuberant to be shy for long, took it. "You and I'll cook a pot of oatmeal that'll make your dad wish he'd waited for breakfast. How about that?"

Penny giggled and started toward the kitchen at Vicky's side. Vicky glanced over her shoulder at me, and I tried to thank her with my eyes.

The phone rang. I went to the hallway alcove and answered it. A business acquaintance was calling. He had read the paper. He was shocked, stunned. If there was anything he could do . . .

I mumbled a thanks for the call. As I hung up, the door chimes sounded.

The caller was Carla Burke. She was a striking woman with a severe type of beauty, tall, long-limbed, her face chiseled in bold, classic lines, her dark brown hair worn in a bun.

"Oh, Steve," she said as she swept into the living room, "I'm terribly broken up about Maureen! I read it in the papers. I know they'll catch the rotter who did it."

"I'm sure they will, Carla," I said. She always made me feel awkward. There was something bold and naked about Carla, even when she was fully clothed.

"Would you like some coffee?" I asked.

"Why not? We have to keep living. Abstinence from a

morning coffee won't bring Maureen back, will it?" She happened to drop a glance at me. "Oh, I'm sorry, Steve. I didn't mean that the way it sounded. I came over to cheer you up, to see if I could be of help."

She kept up a running line of talk as we went into the dining room.

"Have you seen Will?" she asked as she sat down.

"He's in the den asleep."

"Stay here overnight?"

I nodded.

"He might at least have called me," she said. "But that's expecting too much of Will. He never thinks of anything. Steve, you positively must bring Penny and yourself over to the house. You can stay there until all this is over."

"We'll be all right here."

"I insist, Steve. After all, the child needs some protections against the goings-on that must take place."

"Thanks, Carla, but we'll make out."

Her features lost some of their classic evenness. She looked hurt.

The phone rang.

I said, "Excuse me, Carla."

The caller this time was a woman. Shocked, sympathetic. A friend of Maureen's. How could anything so dreadful have happened to a person like Maureen?

My hand was trembling when I replaced the phone.

I was no more back in the dining room when the phone jangled again.

I started to get up. Carla got to her feet before I did.

"I'll catch it, Steve. It's going to be doing that all morning."

For that, I was honestly grateful to her. I hadn't thought ahead that far.

When Carla had left the dining room, I snatched the

38

chance to go into the kitchen. Vicky and Penny had gone outside. I saw them through the window. They were at the picnic table in the back yard having their oatmeal. Vicky was laughing at something Penny had said.

The front door again.

It was a stranger this time, a dark, clean-cut young man dressed neatly in a blue suit.

"Mr. Griffin?"

"Yes."

"I'm Lieutenant Liam Reynolds, Homicide," he said in a soft, low voice. He looked more like a dancer than a cop.

"I guess you want to talk to me," I said.

"Please."

I held the door back for him. "There are some people here already," I said. "There may be more. We can talk in private upstairs."

We went upstairs to the master bedroom. I motioned him to a chair. I sat on the vanity bench.

"I know you want to see him got, Griffin," he said in that easy tone of his, "and got good. I want him—and I'm going to get him. I hope he tries to play his string to the end. He doesn't deserve to reach Headquarters. A jury might let him off with life, and a parole board twenty years from now might let him off for keeps."

He stopped speaking; then he smiled. There was no humor or warmth in it. "Sorry. I've got a wife myself. Same size, same coloring." He stood up, walked to the window. "I talk too much. But I don't like things that crawl out from under rocks and prey on women."

He turned from the view of the lawn below. "Let's start with her phone call to you last night. Was that the first indication you had that she was in trouble?"

I nodded. Reynolds was a surprising man. Looking at him,

I somehow began to feel better. Maybe it was his directness. Suddenly, I realized what a daze I'd been in since last night. At that moment, the fog began to lift. I saw the new day outside. I saw the bed that had supported Maureen's body in sleep. I could say it and believe it now: She was dead, but somebody was going to pay for it.

6

Reynolds returned to his chair, but he didn't sit down. "Your work keeps you away from home most of the time?"

"Yes."

"Then her trouble might have gone back to any date, any time, any event. She could have hidden external signs of being in trouble during the weekends when you were home?"

"I knew her pretty well," I said.

"Don't be defensive, Griffin. I'm not trying to cast any slurs at you or your wife. I take it for granted that you were both fine people. I want that straight. But I want something else made equally straight. A man tried—and succeeded—in killing a woman. It happened that she was your wife, and I'm sorry. But the fact remains: it was a man-woman killing."

I began to burn. I controlled it. He had stated only the simple, blunt truth. "Admitted," I said finally.

"All right. And she might have hidden this trouble from you for a long time? We know that she did keep it hidden for at least a short time. What I'm after is this—could the thing have started months ago? When and where do we start looking? Understand?"

"Yes," I said.

"Well, you haven't answered my question."

"I believe she was too honest to hide anything big from me for long—and that's the truth, Reynolds."

"I believe you. That sort of honesty—it's always coupled with other traits of character, traits that would have made her want to protect you, to keep from you anything that might have brought you grief or harm." Reynolds took a deep breath. "The reason, Griffin. That's what you're afraid of, isn't it?"

"Yes," I said.

"We'll find the reason. Maybe you're right. Maybe the reason was none of her doing at all. Maybe it was only in the mind of the man who killed her."

"I'm sure that's the case, Reynolds."

"She knew the reason, of course, and she knew she couldn't hide it any longer."

"Her phone call to me?"

"That's right. She'd played out her string, reached the point of desperation."

His eyes held mine. I looked away from him. His soft voice followed: "So you see, Griffin, the reason couldn't have been wholly in the mind of the man, after all. You've got to admit that. Admit it without pain, if you can. Admit it without letting it lower her one jot in your mind and heart. We've fenced this thing from every angle. And if we're going to get anywhere you have to admit it. She might have been totally innocent—but something she had done was part of the reason."

I began to see why Reynolds, so young, ranked so high. The man had a mind like an icepick. I had the feeling that as a cop he bordered on that strange phenonemon we call genius.

"Money?" he prodded.

"I don't see how. We have enough to live comfortably. Not so much or so little for it to be dangerous."

"Bad habits?"

"No real vices."

"She drink?"

"Sparingly."

"She ever get tight?"

"Very rarely."

"What constitutes 'rarely' in your opinion, Griffin? Once a month? Once a week? Every New Year's Eve?"

"Now and then at a party, maybe five or six times a year, she'd have a few extra drinks."

"Get staggering, thick in her talk?"

"Never."

"Just a glow," he said.

"Yes."

He waited for several seconds before speaking again. "At those rare times when she was tight—did she get amorous?"

"I don't believe that's any of your business, Reynolds."

"None of this is my business—except catching the man we're after. To that end, anything is my business. I'd expose my own mother to public view if it would mean catching a murderer, Griffin. My mother, and your wife, have my highest consideration as a man. To me as a cop, they are absolute zeros. We're hunting for the reason, and we're going to find it. I want to know how she acted when she was drinking."

"How does any woman act?" I said.

"Don't hedge with me, Griffin. You'll only slow us down. You know damn' well that women act in many different ways. A near prude, with the right edge, can be hell on wheels in bed. I'm not saying your wife did anything. I'm simply asking. Bluntly, I'm wondering. Violent affairs have had their start in a few seemingly innocent drinks when a husband was out of town."

"All right," I said, "I'll tell you. Maureen didn't need liquor. She was a complete woman."

"Thanks. You should have said that right off. Now—was

she the kind to start something—an affair—without a few drinks? From boredom? From loneliness?"

"Positively not. She was too honest for that. If she'd wanted to search other pastures, she'd have told me straight out and I could have taken it or stepped straight to hell. I think you'll have to look for the reason in some tangent to her daily living, Reynolds."

"I'll keep what you say in mind," he said. "Now with your permission, I'd like to take a look through her things. So far we haven't much to go on. A few routine facts. Cause of death: brain injury received, apparently, when a car knocked her down on Timmons Street."

Timmons Street. I hadn't thoroughly read the morning papers and Decoster hadn't told me last night. This was the first knowledge I'd had of exactly where she'd been found. Timmons Street. A dismal, dirty, deserted stretch of waterfront warehouses and flop joints where a room could be had for a dollar.

"She didn't go there alone, on foot," Reynolds said. "The man came here and forced her to go—or talked her into taking a ride with him."

"What do you mean, 'talked' her into it?"

"She called you. Then he came here. Decoster tells me you found the stub of a cigarette he smoked."

"That's right."

"Then they knew each other. Well enough for him to come in, sit down, take a smoke, and persuade her to go out with him."

I got off the vanity bench and walked to the window and looked out at the yard as Reynolds had done. But I knew the yard didn't look the same to me as it had to him.

"They left here together," Reynolds said. "They drove down Timmons Street, toward a destination as yet unknown. On Timmons, she knows this is really it. Maybe she's been talking fast

44

all this while. Now she knows she's reached the end of the line. She fights her way out of the car. He hits her. Uses the car as a weapon."

My brain gave me the dizzying sensation that it was swelling. "It doesn't make sense! Two times before he had tried to hit her with the car. He wanted to use it—as if using the car as a weapon had become a fixation in his mind. Then he comes here, and she lets him in and leaves with him? You believe that? It just doesn't add up!"

"It will—when we learn the reason, when we learn a little more about a lot of things," Reynolds said. "Did she have a place where she kept letters, mementos, bills to be paid?"

"I took care of most of the bills," I said. "Her bookkeeping was erratic. She didn't have any mementos."

"She was an actress once. No scrapbooks?"

I shook my head as I turned to face him. "She said once that she'd clipped every notice and saved every playbill, only to misplace and lose them before they found their way into a scrapbook."

"She handle any money at all?"

"She had a personal checking account. Her checkbook is in the drawer of the bedside table there. I was looking at it last night."

"All in order?"

"I don't know. I was too upset."

"I understand." He moved between the beds and opened the drawer of the small square table. He looked at the checkbook, then handed it to me as I walked over to him.

He watched as I flipped the stubs. "How about it, Griffin?"

A frown creased my forehead. "No, it's not in order. There are too many small ones written to cash lately. The total's out of all proportion to what she usually spends."

"We'll find out who the endorser was." He thrust the checkbook back in the drawer and pulled out the play manuscript I'd seen in there last night.

He thumbed through it. "She tell you she was going to act in a local production?"

"No."

"This thing's written by a man named Randy Price. His name and address are here on the first page. Know him?"

"No."

"We'll go to see him," Reynolds said.

As we went downstairs, I said, "I'll have to make arrangements about my little girl if we're going out."

"Want a policewoman to come over?"

At the foot of the stairway, I hesitated. I didn't want to leave Penny with a policewoman. I had absolutely nothing against policewomen. I admired the work they did. But the one who would come over might be aloof, cold, impersonal. Right now Penny needed more than that. She needed friendliness, someone to take an interest in her and keep her active young mind and body busy, her thoughts off her missing mother.

I thought of Vicky Clayton. True, I'd known her only a brief time, and I was reluctant to leave my child with a stranger. Yet was Vicky really a stranger? There was no doubting the honesty of her feeling over Maureen's death, or of the tenderness in her eyes when she'd first looked at Penny. There was no question of her ability to interest and amuse a child, as she had shown at breakfast.

"A friend of Maureen's is here," I said. "Let me see if she'll stay."

Will Burke was standing in the living room, holding a cup of steaming coffee. He set his cup and saucer on a table. He looked fresh and clear-headed, as if his drinking last night had merely released one of his periodically accumulated heads of steam.

46

He thumbed toward the alcove where Carla was talking on the phone with someone. I introduced him to Reynolds and left the two of them together. Then I went out of the house, through the kitchen. The sun was warm and the sky was a washed-clean blue. Maureen had always loved such a day as this.

7

At the rear of the house I stopped and watched Vicky Clayton and Penny. They had moved over to Penny's sandbox. Vicky sat on the edge of the box, her print dress drawn over her knees and tucked behind her legs. She was building a tiny house of sand, and Penny was watching, serious and absorbed. I told myself it was silly to have any misgivings about leaving Penny in Vicky's care. I was glad Maureen had had such a friend.

As I walked forward, my shadow fell over them. Vicky stood up, looking clean and fine and healthy. Her smile was natural.

"You've brightened her morning immeasurably," I said.

Vicky glanced over her shoulder to see that Penny was busy. "She's wonderful, Steven," she said very softly. "I hope I didn't do anything wrong—but I chatted with her about her mother. I think she's reconciled to her mother's being absent for several days. When she's stopped missing her so much, she can be told some of the truth gradually, without shock."

"You were wise, and I'm deeper in your debt than I thought."

"I love children. I teach, you know."

"No, I didn't."

"Of course—Maureen never mentioned me."

"I'm going out with the detective," I said. "I—I was wondering if you could stay with Penny a little longer. If I'm imposing on your time, please feel free to say so. I could leave Penny with the woman who baby sits for us now and then, but she's too talkative, and I don't like the thought of leaving Penny with a strange policewoman. A child as sensitive as Penny . . ."

"I know what you're trying to say, Steven." Vicky's hand touched mine briefly. "I'd be grateful for the chance to do that little bit for Maureen. Besides, I haven't another claim on my time."

"Fine," I said. "I'll try not to be too long. There are going to be many callers and much to do in the house, I think. Maureen had a lot of friends."

"I'll keep Penny out of the way."

"Good. I'll let Will Burke and his wife take care of visitors."

I looked over Vicky's shoulder. "Penny, on your best behavior with Miss Clayton."

"Yes, Daddy."

I turned and went back to the house. As I opened the backdoor screen, I looked back. Vicky was still standing, watching me. For an instant, she wasn't a part of the bright morning. She wasn't young and unworried. There was a look of suffering in her face. Then she turned quickly and dropped beside Penny.

Reynolds talked little as we drove out of the Meade Park section.

Randy Price's address was on Shady Oak Lane, which was not far from Meade Park, but getting there was like driving into the country.

Shady Oak's history began during the boom between the two wars. At that time, a developer with more ideas than money had visualized a neat middle-class subdivision in the Shady Oak area. Streets had been laid out. Sidewalks had been put in. Lamp standards had been erected. Several lots had been sold and a few cottages built.

Then came the depression. The city grew in other directions, and nature assaulted Shady Oak in an effort to reconquer the area. Now there were stretches of broken sidewalk hidden in weeds. Gaunt, old-fashioned steel lampposts were lonely sentinels, guarding nothing. Between the scattered houses were fields of brush and trees, with a bit of pasture land here and there providing forage for a few cows.

Reynolds and I passed a couple of the small frame houses. They looked as if they hadn't been repaired or painted since the day they were built. Junky cars sat in the yards, and at one house half a dozen small children paused in play to lift their grimy faces long enough to watch our passage.

"That must be the place right ahead," Reynolds said.

Price's house and yard were reasonably neat, and the car beside the cottage was a light, fairly recent model.

The sun was warm, and insects added a lazy hum to the day as Reynolds and I walked across the porch. The lieutenant knocked on the weathered screen door. There was no immediate answer and Reynolds knocked again.

As if coming through a yawn, a voice called from inside, "Okay, okay. Be with you in a second."

Price came to the door and looked at us through the screen. He was young and slender. The lines of his face were fine, sensitive, almost delicate, but they had been cut cleanly. His eyes were dark and alert. He wore his almost-black hair in a butch and would have looked like a teenager had it not been for his small neatly clipped Vandyke and mustache.

"Hi," he said with a grin that showed the flash of large, even white teeth. "Sorry—but I'm not buying anything today."

"And we're not selling anything," Reynolds said.

Price's alert, puppy eyes moved from Reynolds' face to mine.

"You're Randy Price," I said.

50

"That's right, but I don't believe . . ."

"I'm Steve Griffin."

His face lighted with pleasure. "Say now—Maureen's husband? Holy cow, why didn't you let me know you were coming out? I'd have cleaned the joint up."

He held the screen door back and Reynolds and I entered. The small living room held a couple of chairs, desk, a daybed with a faded chintz cover, a straw carpet. Stacks of old books and magazines were at precarious rest on everything except the desk chair and daybed. Randy cleared chairs by the simple expedient of picking up books and magazines and stacking them in a corner.

While he was busy, I had a better chance to look him over. He wore rumpled denim slacks, tee shirt, and house sandals without ankle straps. Slender of frame, his shoulders and elbows were bony; but he moved with the grace and balance of an athlete, his muscles flat, rippling, strong. He was the sort of man who would never go to fat. At fifty-five or sixty he'd still be wiry, ready for a swim after eighteen holes of golf and two fast sets of tennis.

He dusted his hands on his trousers and offered his right hand. "Say, Steve, this is a real pleasure."

His grip was firm. I thought of what Reynolds had said that morning about the reason. Could this boy possibly be the reason? Bored, lonely, could Maureen have . . .

I cut the thought short.

Randy looked me up and down. "Maureen said she was going to have me meet you when you got back to town. Sorry she couldn't come out. Busy, huh?" He turned and shoved a couple of straight wooden chairs toward us. "Look, you guys sit down. Make yourself right at home. I might be able to rustle up a beer."

As we heard him banging around in the kitchen, I glanced at Reynolds.

"Play it dumb," he said. "He doesn't know about Mrs. Griffin."

Randy returned with three moisture-beaded cans of beer and an opener. He set the beer on the desk beside a portable type-writer, opened the cans and handed them around.

I introduced Reynolds as Mr. Reynolds. Randy took it for granted he was a close friend.

As we sat, sipping beer out of the cans, a fresh breeze came billowing through the cottage.

"Do you share Maureen's interest in the theater, Steve?"

"I'm afraid I don't know much about things theatrical. My life is a little more mundane."

Randy laughed indulgently. "Well, it takes all kinds to keep the world clicking along. But you've missed one of the most exciting things in life."

"The theater, in a roundabout way, brought me Maureen," I reminded him.

"Say now, that's good! I know all about the way you met. She was in the USO and you were in the army. But even I never interpreted it quite that way."

Randy tipped his beer can to his mouth, and we were silent while he drank. He wiped his mouth with the back of his hand. "Of course," he said, "I'm a long way from the theater yet. But I'm learning. Studying life and people, which are the only sources of great theater. I'm reading, studying, working. Incessantly."

A light began to burn in his eyes. "Great theater happens when a great truth, a great experience, is sharpened and compressed to two hours or more of acting time. It takes a great deal to reach that."

I could easily understand how this boy might instantly seal a friendship with Maureen. He was intense, eager, enveloped in a dream that had once touched her briefly. The dream was the most important thing in the world to him. It was so real that he probably didn't realize the poverty of the cottage and the loneliness of its surroundings.

A woman with Maureen's impulsive generosity and kindness would have wanted to help him the moment she glimpsed his dream. A hard-headed businessman might argue that Randy was fleeing from reality. But Maureen would never have seen the boy that way. She'd have seen his grace and spirit and would have admired him for doing what he felt driven to do regardless of what the world might think. He might even have aroused in her a lonely regret, a ghost of guilt, a haunted feeling that she, unlike Randy, had lacked the necessary something required to hold onto the dream.

"I'll never be able to repay your wife, Steve," Randy said. "She has a natural sense of theater, of what will play and what will not. More important, she understands to some extent what I'm trying to do. It's a rare quality in this rough, tough commercial world. Perhaps some day I can write her into a play and make her immortal." He was deadly serious; then he flashed me a smile. "If that's not too presumptuous of me."

"Not at all," I said.

"I'm writing plays, plays, plays," he said. "And then rewriting them. Attacking every scene, every line, every nuance of feeling from every angle. I've got a trunkful of them. When I get several that please me, I'm going to New York. I know," he said with such stark frankness and simplicity that I almost believed him, "that I'll be famous. I have it—the extra ounce of awareness of life and people. The world will some day recognize what Maureen and a few others see clearly today."

He stopped speaking, a shy smile appearing. The smile took the sharp edge of egotism from his statement without undermining its seriousness. I had never before seen such superb, simple self-confidence.

"Say," Randy said into the little silence his words had brought, "you guys need more beer?"

"No, thanks," I said.

"Still have some," Reynolds answered.

Randy leaned back, stretched his legs before him, and crossed them. "Couple weeks ago, when I met Maureen, I had no idea what a lucky break it was. She still knows a few people. She's going to get some of my better stuff in the hands of a good agent."

"We have one of your plays in the car," Reynolds said. "Perhaps Mrs. Griffin intended to show it to the agent."

"Well, she has three of them." A frown came to Randy's face. "Why'd she give you the play?"

His glance moved between Reynolds and me. "Steve, why'd Maureen send the play out here like this? Is she ill?"

"No."

"It couldn't be because of you," Randy said. "From all she's told me about you—you're just not the type to be so narrow-minded as to think . . ."

"Of course not."

"Then what in the hell is it?" he demanded. His eyes narrowed. "This isn't a purely social call."

"I'm afraid not," Reynolds said. "As matter of fact, Mr. Price, I'm a policeman."

Randy's eyes were wide again, his face a blank. "I don't get this."

"When did you see Mrs. Griffin last?"

"Steve," Randy cried, "what is it? Has something happened to her?"

"Just answer my question," Reynolds said.

"Look, you guys, if something's happened, I have a right— Yesterday afternoon at her house— How about telling me . . ."

"What time?"

"How should I know? I don't run my life by a clock. Two o'clock. Three o'clock maybe. Maybe even later. I'd been to town to pick up some typing paper. I was nearby, so I stopped. She said she had a headache and still had her shopping to do at the supermarket. I offered to go for her, but she said no. I left right away."

"Came straight home?"

"Picked up a few cans of beer. Will you please tell me—"

"Then what did you do?"

"Cooked some eggs, ate, drank a beer, sat down at the desk, put paper in typewriter. I want to know—"

"How long did you work?"

"I don't know. I don't time myself. I worked until I got tired. Then I flopped on the bed and went to sleep."

"How did you happen to meet Mrs. Griffin?"

"Steve, hasn't Maureen told you about it?"

"No," I said.

"I asked you a question," Reynolds said mildly.

"Look, Steve," Randy implored, "who is this guy? Why is he here? What could I have possibly done . . ."

Reynolds cleared his throat.

"All right," Randy said. "First time I saw Maureen was right here."

"In this cottage?" Reynolds said in surprise.

"Of course not! She was using Shady Oak as a cutoff between her house and Fairhill Turnpike."

"What's on Fairhill?" Reynolds asked.

"Dudley Loudermilk," I said. "A fellow who does yard work for us now and then."

"That's right," Randy said. "She did say something about seeing a yard man. Anyhow, she was in trouble. Know what brought our friendship into being? A broken fan belt on her car. A little thing like that, happening in just the right spot at the exact time. The finger of Destiny, reaching down to touch a fan belt."

"We'll discuss Destiny later," Reynolds said. "Right now we're talking about Mrs. Griffin."

"It was simple enough," Randy said. "People never think of

a fan belt until it breaks, and that's usually a million miles from nowhere."

"Her car was on Shady Oak?"

"Yes, about half a mile from the house. A real tired horse, steaming like a calliope. She said she was afraid to try driving it farther and had remembered passing a cottage, my cottage. I saw her from the doorway, the first time. She was walking up Shady Oak. Very nice looking and very tired. Not dressed for a walk out here. Just came as if she were walking out of nowhere, right up to this cottage."

8

Randy looked out the front door as if he expected to see her coming up the walk all over again. "She wanted to use a phone to get a tow car. I don't have a phone; I won't have one. I'd tear it out by the roots if it jangled at me while I was working. I told her I had a car and would be glad to help her."

He was still looking at the screen, and I turned, with the eerie feeling that she might be standing there. I could visualize the charm of her as she'd stood there, warm from her walk, her grin a little crooked.

"So you took her to her car?" Reynolds said.

"Not right off," Randy answered. "She was tired from the hike, especially since she'd made it in spike-heeled shoes. I offered her a glass of water. She really needed it. She accepted it, and we chatted for a few moments, here in the front room. When she saw the typewriter and the manuscript of a play on my desk, our talk switched to the theater. In five minutes or so we were old friends.

"We went out to my car, and the blasted thing wouldn't start. It's not a real old model, but it was a taxicab; I got it cheap, and sometimes it's balky. Well, we had a real laugh. She wasn't impatient, as most women would have been. I finally got my crate started and we drove to her car and she told me I must visit her and her husband. As she drove away, I knew that something fine and wonderful had happened. Now for the last time will you tell me why all the questions, what this is all about?"

"Mrs. Griffin is dead," Reynolds said.

"Dead?" Price whispered the word.

Reynolds nodded.

Randy was so pale his skin looked waxen. "I don't believe you," he said. "It can't be true." He looked in my eyes for an instant, then turned his face away.

"When?" he said.

"Last night," Reynolds answered.

"Just like that?" Randy asked. "People don't go off that way unless they're sick or something. She wasn't. She was the most vital, healthy person I've ever known."

"She was run over by a car," Reynolds said. "It happened on Timmons Street."

The boy sat perfectly still. Then his face began to twist. His chin trembled, and the Vandyke was suddenly ridiculous. His eyes filled with tears.

"How could it have happened to her?" he whispered. "How could it? What'll I do?"

"What will *you* do?" Reynolds echoed. "You might think of her and Mr. Griffin."

"I'll never forget her," Randy said. "I'm sorry, Steve. I was thinking of my work; this is a shock to me. I must do as she would want. Learn from this. Taste life in the midst of death. Let it mature me. Rise above it. Work harder than ever. Mustn't I?"

I looked away from him and stared at the gritty old carpet. "Yes, Randy, I guess you must."

Randy sat with his hands covering his face. Then he looked up. A new thought had come to him. "Timmons Street. . . . What was she doing there?"

"We think she was taken there," I said.

"Deliberately? Forced to go?"

"Yes."

"Then it wasn't an accident!"

"No."

"Somebody killed her on purpose?" The thought brought him to his feet. A hard pulse was jolting in his throat.

"That's the way it looks," I said.

"Who did it? Who *would* do it?"

"We don't know yet," Reynolds said. He stood, hands in his pockets. "Whoever he was, he had made two earlier attempts on her life, with a car very similar to the Griffin family car. You know anyone else who has a heavy green sedan like the Griffin car?"

"No," Randy said.

"Did she mention that anybody was out to get her?"

Randy's face twisted in pain. " 'Out to get her'? No, she didn't say anything like that, but I had the feeling yesterday that something was bothering her. I asked, but she just said she hadn't been feeling well, not sick or anything, just sort of in the dumps. The headache explanation seemed okay to me."

"You were here all last night?"

"I've told you that, Mr. Reynolds."

"Alone."

"Yes. If I'm supposed to have an alibi, I'm out of luck. I didn't know I'd need one." He turned to me. "When will the funeral be?"

"Day after tomorrow, I think."

"I'll be there. If you need me for anything, let me know."

"Thanks, Randy, I will."

He followed us to the door.

"I'm sorry we had to meet under these circumstances, Steve."

"So am I."

"Steve—"

"Yes?"

"She loaned me a little money. I'll pay it back as soon as—"

"We can talk about that some other time."

He nodded and fumbled a cigarette out of his pocket. We left him standing there, a superb young animal, but forlorn.

Reynolds and I drove for a while in silence. At last he said, "I don't like him."

I glanced across the car seat at him. "Why not?"

"I don't know. I see a person now and then who makes me think, 'I wouldn't want you coming up behind my back.' Too long a cop, I guess. Too much looking for opposites in people."

"Opposites?"

"By the time they reach maturity, many people show the world a shell, a false pod for the real seed. They show a picture of what they want to believe they are. If you look close enough, you can see behind the mask."

"That isn't always true. I don't believe it was true in my wife's case."

"I didn't know your wife, Griffin. But I know that boy. Even while he was crying, I kept picturing him in my mind with his lips curled in contempt of everything beneath his own fancied genius."

"What could he have to do with Maureen's death?"

"I didn't say he had anything to do with it. I simply said I didn't like him."

Reynolds changed the subject. "There are some papers at Headquarters I want you to sign."

"Papers?"

"Okaying an autopsy," he said.

I nodded. I'd read a description of an autopsy once. I didn't

60

like to think about it happening to anybody. This one would be done on Maureen.

We drove to Headquarters and I signed the papers, almost refusing at the final moment. I didn't see what good an autopsy would do. We knew how she'd been killed.

We came down the corridor in police Headquarters and turned in at Reynolds' office. It was a small room, furnished with the usual desk, chairs, and filing cabinet. A light with a green shade hung from the ceiling on a long wire. Two men were in the office, smoking cigarettes and chatting. Each of them said hello to Reynolds when we came in. One was a short, meek-looking man, the other of average size, and sandy-haired, who appeared to be in his mid-thirties.

"These are two of our men," Reynolds said. "Lamb and Swain."

We shook hands. Swain was the taller, younger one.

"Anything on Timmons Street?" Reynolds asked.

"Not yet," Swain said. "We combed the area."

"No witnesses."

"No."

"There wouldn't be—down there. It isn't etiquette on Timmons Street to talk to a cop. But stay with it. Pull in the known barflies. Throw a vag charge at them. You might hit one who wants to talk his way out of jail."

Lamb and Swain picked up their hats, murmured expressions of sympathy to me, and went out.

Reynolds moved around his desk and sat down. "I'll send you home in a squad car, Griffin."

I nodded.

He looked up at me. "Can you take some more legwork?"

"If it's necessary."

"I think it is. I want you as close to this investigation as possible. A chance word or action might crop up somewhere that would seem okay to us, but which you—knowing her—would spot as being out of line."

"I'll get some lunch," I said.

"Good. I'll pick you up at your house in about an hour." He flipped an intercom switch on his desk. A heavy voice said, "Desk."

"Charlie, tell Mallory I want him to take Mr. Griffin home."

"Will do."

In a few moments, a young, fresh-faced cop came into the office. He was Mallory, and we went out together.

We got in a squad car in the parking lot behind the city building. Mallory was respectful, and his attitude expressed sympathy. Otherwise, he was as silent and remote as a big shaggy, sleepy dog.

I watched traffic stream past us.

"I'd like to detour by Timmons Street," I said.

"You want to see the place where it happened?"

I nodded.

And he nodded in return and turned at the next corner.

9

If there were morbidity and despair in the impulse to swing by Timmons Street, they were based on the haunting wish that I could have been there at the very end, to have done something to avert the end.

My muscles tightened and my forehead grew damp as we neared Timmons Street. The character of the city had undergone a change as we moved from the healthy bustle uptown to this end of town. Traffic thinned, and the nearly deserted sidewalks lay sooty along littered gutters. The few pedestrians slouched along, as if each moved in his own private domain of broken dreams. A damp, sour smell seeped off the river to envelop secondhand stores and greasy restaurants and poolrooms.

We turned into Timmons.

It was a short street that stretched for several blocks between two others that dead-ended at a river wharf. On the right side was an almost continuous wall of dirty brick and warped planking—warehouses with their faces to the river. Between every second or third warehouse an alley snaked off Timmons to a dock. To my left were gloomy, deserted stores, another poolroom, a hash house, smaller warehouses, and flop joints. On the corner was a mission. An old bum stood outside, worrying his hat in his hand as he tried to make up his mind to go in and try for a meal.

Mallory stopped the car.

"Right over here," he said quietly.

We got out and Mallory walked ahead of me. When we had moved down the street a few paces, I saw the chalk marks the police had made in the street: head, feet, legs, arms, all drawn there; the empty outline of a warm-fleshed woman who had worried if I didn't eat right, if I had a cold, or if I were tired from a trip; who'd lain in my arms and given fully of herself.

I turned from the spot, my throat so dry my breath rasped against it.

I looked at the face of the dirty street again. Timmons never completely slept. There was always a wino huddled in a doorway or a pair of them squeezing Sterno in an alley or a man wandering into a flophouse or an old bag with nothing left to sell crawling to the mission for the night.

Suspicion and fear were never far from Timmons.

A heavy green sedan would have been noticed.

If not, her scream would have been heard.

I stood there hating every bum on the street. One of them must have seen. One of these faceless, nameless, gray-skinned shadows could tell the cops enough for a start. But no one on Timmons Street talked to cops.

"This is where her body was found," Mallory said. "To judge from the position and angle, she must have been over here when he hit her."

We walked toward the right and back up the street a little way. I stood where she would have stood. It was night, and she was standing there with his headlights coming full at her. She was shaky and weak. She'd just picked herself up from the street where he'd thrown her from the car. The clash and grind of the gears was still in her ears: reverse, forward. Her mouth opened to scream as she heard the high, fast snarl of the motor.

She turned to run. She was able to take two or three steps. Then she'd been hurled over there, and it was as if she'd never been. Only a few chalk marks on the pavement. Not even skid marks, because he hadn't been trying to stop. He'd been trying to hit her.

A weird silence had come over the street. It was as if the very buildings were watching me and resenting me. The street would never give up its secret. Then the silence was broken by the deep bass of a tug on the river. I turned and looked down the alley at it. It was moving upriver, toward midstream. It had brought in a scabrous barge which seamen were now mooring at the end of the old dock. The dock served, according to a weathered sign, a warehouse belonging to Kukolovitch and Sons.

Activity on the barge was coming to a standstill. The three seamen, in jeans and turtle-neck sweaters, were watching me, one of them still with a hawser in his hand.

It occurred to me what a strange figure I must present, a man in a business suit standing in the middle of Timmons Street with a crazy look on his face.

I turned toward the squad car. Mallory seemed to relax as I got in. "Thanks," I said.

"You just had to get it out of your system," he said.

When I reached my home, it had a feeling of emptiness. Then Vicky Clayton came out of the kitchen.

"Hello, Steven," she said. "I was just fixing some lunch."

"I'm not very hungry. Penny give you any trouble?"

She smiled. "Are you kidding? If the world was full of Pennys there wouldn't be much trouble for anyone. We had a fine morning. Right now she's upstairs cleaning up for lunch."

"Many people come by?"

"A steady stream. Mr. Burke got rid of the last of them half an hour ago. He called his office and said he had to get down

65

there for a while. He said that you could reach him there if you needed him and that he would drop in later to stay as long as necessary."

"Did Carla leave with him?"

"Mrs. Burke? Yes, they left together."

I dropped tiredly on the living-room couch.

"You need a cup of hot black coffee," Vicky said.

"I guess I do."

"I've got sandwiches all made."

"Okay, lead me on."

"That's better, Steven. For a minute there you looked as if you wanted to—relax."

"That isn't the word you started to say."

Her eyes met mine directly. She had honest eyes, well spaced, steady. "I was about to use the word 'quit,' " she admitted.

"I was on Timmons Street," I said.

She paled. "You shouldn't have—but then, I guess you had to, didn't you?"

"Yes."

"I think we'd better eat, Steven."

Penny came down the stairs in a rush. She slowed as she reached the dining room and bounced into her chair with some slight semblance of being a lady. "Hullo, Daddy. Vicky and I watched ants this morning."

"You did?"

"We saw them marching and carrying bread crumbs into their holes," Penny said.

We ate to the accompaniment of Penny's chatter. Finally she had finished and resigned herself to taking an afternoon nap. Vicky went upstairs with her and returned as I was finishing a cup of coffee. We cleared the table together, carried the stacks of dishes to the kitchen. As she ran hot water into the sink, Vicky said, "I'm looking for work, Steven."

66

"I thought you said you teach."

"I do. But there's no school right now. Remember? School doesn't run twelve months out of the year. I have loads of time and I've been wondering what to do with myself."

She added detergent to the hot water. "You haven't had a chance to think about it yet, but finding the right person to keep house and take care of Penny isn't going to be easy. Please, let me help. For a few days at least. Until you have a chance to begin setting your life in order again."

"I'd be very glad to have you do that, Vicky."

"Thanks, Steven. Will you give me those cups?"

I handed them to her. "In many ways you're like her."

"Maureen?"

"Yes," I said. "You have the same sort of kindness and generosity."

She turned her face away and was silent for a few moments. Then she said, in a carefully controlled voice, "May I take Penny to dinner this evening and perhaps to a movie?"

"If you like."

"I'm thinking of what's best for her, Steven. I don't want her to grow suspicious of the way I'm keeping her out of the house, but I want to avoid the people who may come calling. She's sensitive, and she's sure to feel something is terribly wrong. I thought we'd have an afternoon of shopping, visit a park, then have dinner and go to a movie."

"You'll wear her out."

"That's what I'm hoping," she said with a faint smile. "May I?"

"Of course."

Reynolds arrived at the house a few minutes later. He was driving a black, unmarked car. As we drove off I asked, "Where are we going?"

"To the spots where he tried and failed."

"The plant nursery and supermarket?"

Reynolds nodded. "She was a regular customer at both places?"

"Yes."

"That'll help. It won't be like asking questions about a stranger."

The Green Thumb was on the south edge of town. The establishment consisted of a white frame office, a pair of long glass greenhouses, and acres of plants. It was run by a plump, merry old lady, her son, and two daughters. The girls, in their early twenties, were working beyond the office, setting up sprinklers. Mrs. Judson and her son were in the workroom behind the office making up corsages.

Mrs. Judson took my hand between both of hers. "I read it in the papers, Mr. Griffin. . . ." Her usually bright face became sad.

Her son, a thin youth in his late teens, stood shyly by. "We're very sorry, Mr. Griffin."

"Thanks," I said.

"She was such a good woman," Mrs. Judson said.

"She thought highly of you, too, Mrs. Judson. I want you to meet this gentleman. Mr. Reynolds. He's a detective and wants to ask you some questions."

"I hope we can be of some help."

"I hope so, Mrs. Judson," Reynolds said. "You see, someone tried to run Mrs. Griffin down twice before. Once right outside the nursery here. Just a couple of days ago."

Mrs. Judson's face whitened. Her eyes went round, leaving tears like forgotten jewels on their lower lids.

"Do you remember her coming here that recently, Mrs. Judson?"

"Oh, yes."

"And did you see anything happen when she left?"

"No. She told me what she wanted—some plants to set out. She took some bulbs, and I said we'd deliver the cuttings when the ground was prepared and she was all ready for them. She just went out. I didn't see a thing unusual. I had no earthly idea . . ."

"Of course you didn't," Reynolds said. "How about your daughters?"

"If I remember aright, they were both downtown."

"And your son?"

"I was probably in the workroom making up funeral wreaths," he said. "Anyway, I remember being in back when Mrs. Griffin came in. I stuck my head out just long enough to say hello while she and Mom talked here in the display room. I didn't see her leave."

Reynolds said, "Thanks—and forgive the intrusion."

Mrs. Judson followed us to the door. "I just wish there was something we could do. Mr. Griffin—do you still want the cuttings?"

I nodded. Reynolds and I got back in the car.

"Bad break," he said, starting the motor. "Maybe we'll do better at the supermarket."

10

We drove to the supermarket on the edge of Meade Park. It was a big concrete and glass store, briskly and brightly modern. Reynolds and I asked one of the white-uniformed attendants for the manager, and he led us up a short flight of stairs to a low-ceiling office that overlooked the long checking lanes from one angle and the sweeping interior of the store from another.

The manager's name was Ordway. He was young, on the shy side of thirty, I guessed. Brisk and erect, a young executive type with alert eyes.

"Some complaint, gentlemen?"

"No," Reynolds said. "Just questions. I'm a policeman."

Ordway looked at him without expression.

"Did you know a Mrs. Griffin who traded here regularly?" Reynolds asked.

"Yes. Terrible thing. I read in the paper about what happened to her. Reminded me of her last visit here."

"What happened then?" Reynolds asked.

"Why, she was almost killed—right out there on the street."

"Did you see it?" I broke in.

"This is Mr. Griffin," Reynolds explained.

70

"Oh—I'm sorry, Mr. Griffin," Ordway said. "No, I didn't see it happen."

"Then how did you know about it?" Reynolds asked.

"I heard some of the employees, a group of them, down front. They were quite excited. I went down to see what the trouble was. They told me Mrs. Griffin had almost had an accident. They went back to work, and I didn't think of it again—until I read the newspapers."

"If you didn't see it," Reynolds said, "who did?"

"I don't know."

"Someone did, or they wouldn't have been talking about it."

"Then let's find out," Ordway said. He got up and went quickly down the short flight of stairs, Reynolds and I close behind him.

The third employee we spoke to was a plump brunette. She was a checker, and stood with her back to her cash register as we talked. Customers with food carts in nearby lines watched curiously.

"You remember when Mrs. Griffin almost had her accident, of course," Ordway said.

"Gee, yes, Mr. Ordway."

"Did you see it?"

"No, but I was the first he told about it."

"Who?" Reynolds put in.

"Tommy. Tommy Haines. He saw it."

Reynolds glanced at the manager.

"Tommy is a stock clerk," Ordway said. "When we have long lines out here he bags purchases and carries them out to our customers' cars. He's in back now, helping unload a shipment of tomatoes."

We went to the stockroom. It was cool and dim, cluttered with crates, boxes, baskets. It smelled of earth and winy apples.

A trailer truck was backed up to the wide overhead doors. A man was inside, handing crates of tomatoes to a man standing at the rear of the truck just inside the stockroom. The second man was stacking the crates on a hand dolly. Lounging against the handles of the dolly was a tall gangling youth.

"Tommy," Ordway said. "Will you come over here a moment?"

The youth broke off his conversation with the dolly loader and came toward us.

Ordway introduced us. Tommy wiped his hands on his white apron and shook hands.

"Mr. Reynolds wants to ask you some questions about Mrs. Griffin," Ordway said.

"All right, sir," Tommy said. "I'll do the best I can."

"You saw Mrs. Griffin yesterday?" Reynolds said.

"Yes, sir. It's a policy of the store to be able, if you can, to greet regular customers by name. We've known Mrs. Griffin a long time. She came here yesterday and got some groceries. It was in the afternoon rush period. I bagged them and carried them outside for her. It was near closing time, and there were a lot of cars in the parking area. She'd parked on the street, the other side of the street.

"She thanked me and took the package when we reached the sidewalk. I offered to take the groceries across, but she said that would be okay, it was a small package. So she started across and I started to go back to the store. Then it happened!" Tommy made an explosive gesture with his hand. "I heard her yell. I turned and looked. She'd caught a good break in traffic, to make the crossing. But there was this car that must have whipped out of the intersection. It was going fast, and whoever was driving must have lost his head when she yelled like that."

"What do you mean?"

"Well, she'd dropped the groceries and she was getting out

72

of the way—fast. But instead of cutting away from her, the guy got rattled and cut toward her. Then, right at the last second, he yanked the wheel and swerved away from her."

"You're sure of that?"

"It looked that way. It was all happening so fast."

"I understand."

"Well, it was a lucky thing she was young and quick. If she'd been an old lady, it would have been curtains. She never would've got out of the way in time. When I saw she was okay, first thing I thought was what if I'd carried them groceries on out there? I might not have seen the guy quick as she did.

"I ran out and helped her get up. She'd tripped, see, and fallen to her knees, but only after the guy was past. Just like her legs had collapsed. She said she was all right and didn't want a doctor. She was going home, she said. When she saw her husband, she said, everything would be all right."

"She got in her car and drove away then?"

"Yeah. And the funny thing was that she was driving a car just like the one that nearly hit her."

"How about the license number, Tommy?"

"Gosh, I didn't think of that until the guy had gone around the next corner and was out of sight."

"You're sure a man was driving?"

"Looked like a man."

"Could it have been a woman with, say, an Italian haircut?"

"Never thought of that. Could have been. Just figured it was a man."

"Get a good look at him?"

"Nope. Just what you'd expect. Just somebody driving the car."

"Did she say anything to you about the car or driver?"

"Nope. She was crying a little. That didn't surprise me. She was mumbling. Didn't make a lot of sense. Just words."

"Can you remember them?"

"She was crying and mumbling at the same time. She said she wanted her husband. That figured. Then she said she had to reach somebody, but it was like she wasn't talking about reaching her husband."

"What do you mean?"

"Well," Tommy said, scratching his sandy head, "she'd said she was going to reach her husband. Then when she said she had to reach this particular somebody, she said it in a different way."

"As if she were talking about someone else?"

"That's right, Mr. Reynolds. She said she had to reach him and let him know he was wrong. She wasn't wrong. She'd been wrong. But she wasn't wrong now. It was him that was wrong now. She hadn't meant any of it and he was wrong. Just words. Kind of hysterical, you know."

"Thanks, Tommy."

"Sure." He grinned at the store manager. "Glad to get away from them tomatoes for a few minutes. I guess the lady was okay once she got home to her husband."

"Then you haven't read the papers?" I asked.

"Nah. Your wife *is* all right, ain't she, Mr. Griffin?"

"I'm afraid not, Tommy," I said.

"You mean . . ."

"Yesterday afternoon was the second time he'd tried to hit her with the car. Last night he tried again."

Tommy gulped. "And the third time . . . ?"

I nodded.

"Gee, Mr. Griffin, I'm sorry. I didn't mean—"

"You've been a great help, Tommy. Thanks very much."

Reynolds and I left Tommy and Ordway staring after us. We squeezed around the rear corner of the trailer and tractor job, leaving through the rear. Outside, we walked around the building and got into the car. Reynolds was a deft, sure driver. We threaded swiftly through traffic.

Somewhere *he* might be driving safely and securely through traffic at this moment. A dozen blocks away. Or in another city. Even another state. In a nation on wheels, how do you pluck the right man from the right car and smash him until he's as lifeless as that thing he left on Timmons Street?

"Relax, Griffin."

"What?"

"Take it easy."

"That's easy to say, Reynolds."

"I know. But brooding isn't going to help things. A brooding mind is a shadowed mind, and a shadowed mind is inefficient. We've come a long way on this thing."

"Have we?" I asked bitterly.

"We work on cases sometimes for months, years. She was killed only last night. Already we know several things."

"Such as?"

"The car. A twin to yours, Griffin." Reynolds turned a corner. "She remarked on it. So did Tommy Haines."

"Could be a coincidence, after all. He might just happen to own that kind of car."

"Maybe. But if it's coincidence, it's a broad one. That particular shade of green isn't common; neither is the make of car."

We'd bought the sedan for that reason. Maureen had wanted something different. Not flashy, just unusual.

"I think we're dealing with a nut," Reynolds said. "Everything points to it. He took a long chance on somebody seeing him well enough for future identification or on getting his license number when he tried that stunt in front of a busy supermarket. He's thinking in patterns that are violently abnormal.

"Suppose for a minute that he has a fixation that the job had to be done with a certain kind of car—a car like yours. It might point to the reason, Griffin. We've racked our brains for the reason, but the use of the car as a weapon might have been pointing at it the whole time. Why should he use a car just like yours?"

I stared at Reynolds.

His face was tight. "I suspect you're a jump ahead of my reasoning. The car, in his mind, has a significance. There is only one possible significance—your car had done something to him!"

"That's crazy!"

"Maybe. The whole thing is crazy. We're working on the assumption that we're dealing with a crazy man."

"If there'd been any kind of accident, Maureen would have reported it," I said. "She'd have told me."

"Maybe," he said again. "Maybe not. If she had hurt someone, she might have panicked. Anyway, I didn't say she was driving. Do you ever lend the car?"

"We've never made a practice of it."

"You've remarked on her generosity, her impulsive kindness, time and again, Griffin. If someone had needed the car, would she have loaned it?"

"We're pretty careful about that kind of thing," I said. "Anyhow, all the people we know have cars. They wouldn't need ours."

"They might. Randy Price, for example. If he ever writes a smash hit, he'll probably buy himself a pink and gold Caddy. Right now he's driving an ex-taxicab, an unreliable junk heap. If he had car trouble, she would have loaned him yours."

"She might have."

"So your car is taken out and whoever is driving it does something that triggers the paranoid tendencies of this nut we're after. He doesn't stop to wonder who was driving your car. Somehow he traces it. He sees her in it. He goes out and buys a car just like it—and kills her with it."

I shivered.

"Has your car been repaired recently?" Reynolds asked. "Bent fender? Broken headlight? Anything like that?"

"Not that I know of."

"We'll find out. It'll take time. He's built himself a tight house, Griffin. Nobody knows him. Nobody can identify him. Nobody as yet knows his real reason. But tight as the house is, he left the garage door open when he used that car. . . ."

11

I had dinner in town. Afterward, I walked the streets for a long while. I was exhausted, but there was a pressure, a driving force, in me that was not to be resisted.

I tried to remember what it was like to be a living human being. I had been one yesterday, right up to the time of her phone call. The call had rung down a curtain. It had happened a lifetime ago, casting the shadow of unreality over my world. I tried to recall how she looked when she laughed and talked, but all I could think of was her body in the morgue.

I went into a bar and had two stiff drinks, double Scotches. They didn't help much. In some people, the mood prior to a drink determines what the drink will do for them. I was in the wrong mood to start drinking. I listened to the laughter and talk in the bar. I looked at the faces, and when I began to resent them and hate them, I felt frightened.

I left the bar, whistled down a taxi, and went home.

The house was dark. Of course. Vicky had taken Penny out for the evening.

I began to tremble when I entered the quiet, dark living room. I had an urge to run out of the house. I didn't know where.

I sat on the couch and forced myself to breathe deeply, until the smothering sensation went out of my chest.

There was a lot of living still to be done in the house. It was Penny's house too. I must never forget that again.

I started up the dark stairs. Now that I had a grip on myself, I began to realize how tired I really was. I'd lie down, for a little while, until Vicky and Penny came home.

The bedroom door was half open. I pushed inside the room and reached for the light switch. I didn't complete the gesture.

I stood looking at the little firefly.

That was my first thought. There was a firefly, here in the bedroom. Hovering steadily in one spot beside the head of the bed.

The pinpoint glow winked out.

If I hadn't been a smoker myself, I'd have smelled the aroma still lingering in the room. He'd heard me coming up the stairs and had crushed out the cigarette hurriedly. I'd seen the final glow of it. I knew he was still in here. As I moved for the light again, I heard the intake of his breath, the rustle of his clothing.

He hit me savagely on the side of the head. The darkness was filled with technicolor lights for an instant. As I folded toward the floor, he struck down at me. He missed my head but almost broke my left shoulder. As I made a feeble grab for him, I touched the cloth of his trousers. He kicked. The toe of his shoe caught me under the point of the chin; my head snapped and my body rolled backward. I was vaguely aware of him bending over me. Faintly, I could hear the rasp of his breathing. After an instant's hesitation his fingers wandered over my head, my face, as if searching for blood. I wasn't sure whether he had broken the skin.

With an effort of will, I tried to clear my head, tried to force strength into my arms and legs, tried to grapple with him. He beat my pawing hands aside. His fingers dug into the shoulders

79

of my jacket; then, with a swift, deft motion, he shoved backward and downward, smashing the back of my head against the floor. Pain swelled in the back of my skull. I opened my mouth against the pressure, to keep from blacking out.

Again I could feel his hands on my head and face. They explored my pockets. Then I had the sensation that he had straightened and moved back from me.

He was thinking, considering something. It seemed the room was filled with the swift, wild surge of his thoughts.

I tried to drag myself away. I managed to turn my body and claw for a grip on the carpet. Again his fingers twisted in my hair. He was quiet, merciless, and savage. He banged the back of my head once more against the floor.

I was numb, vague. It was a dream that was happening to someone else. The room tilted and turned slowly. My arms were being pulled, stretched far beyond their normal reach. Then my arms fell forward, like detached parts of what had once been me. My face pressed against a surface that was solid and hard and cold. Like the tile on the floor of our bathroom.

Now he had turned away from me and was searching for something in the darkness. There was a rattling of bottles, as if he were feeling around in the medicine cabinet over the washbasin.

Then I was being hauled around again, sideways. He was draping my arms over the edge of the bathtub. Suddenly I felt the rough cloth of a bath towel pulled tight across my face. I tried to lift my hands. But the towel seemed a great distance above my reach.

He was leaning against me, with his knee in the middle of my back, holding my body firmly against the outside rim of the tub. As I lay, legs crumpled under me on the tile floor, head and arms draped across the lip of the tub, he bent over me and pulled my limp arm toward him slightly. With his other hand he was feeling my wrist, the inner side of my wrist, searching for the vein.

And then I understood. He had been looking in the medicine cabinet for a razor blade. He had found it, and was reaching forward to use it. He was going to make it appear that a grief-stricken husband had slashed his wrists, taken his own life. Soon I would feel the bite of the blade; the gush of warm life pulsing from my wrist into the white coldness of the tub.

A ragged moan tore past my lips, and I began writhing beneath the pressure of his knee and the weight of his body. I felt his knee slip. Off balance, he released my wrist to keep from falling over me. I pulled myself around and tried to crawl out of the bathroom. The towel tore loose, and I gasped for air.

He remained quick and sure. Desperate, but controlling himself, he knew that he still had me; he knew that the creature floundering in the darkness couldn't escape him if he took his time. He could still make it look like suicide if he didn't mark me.

Somewhere a door slammed.

Everything in the bathroom stopped. The air itself became static. I was afraid to move. After a moment or so I realized I was alone in the bathroom. I hadn't heard him go out. I had no way of seeing him. But I knew he had slipped into the bedroom.

I heard someone laugh downstairs. The bedroom door was still standing open as I'd left it, and the sound drifted up quite clearly. Then it was cut off as he softly closed the door. A window whispered in its casing. A breath of moist, cool air touched my face as I crawled to the bathroom doorway.

The window slid closed, and he was gone.

I heard Penny and Vicky outside in the hallway. They were going toward Penny's room, saying something about the little rabbit in the cartoon, and Donald Duck.

I guessed that my visitor was at the bottom of the trellis by now, moving through the darkness over the yard, vanishing into the black mouth of night.

I lay with my eyes closed until strength came back to me. A splitting pain began to furrow my brain. I held to the jamb of the bathroom doorway and pulled myself to my feet. I began to feel sick to my stomach. I lit the light, then made it over to the medicine cabinet. It was standing open, as he had left it. I fumbled for the bottle of aspirin. The pills shook themselves into my palm, once I got the bottle open. I swallowed four of the little white pellets and chased them with two glasses of water.

I blinked to focus my eyes, then looked at myself in the bathroom mirror. There was a slight swelling on the upper side of my head where he'd hit me the first time. Other than that, I was unmarked.

I turned and looked at the tub: the big white basin that was to have caught my blood.

A light rapping sounded on the bedroom door. "Steven?"

"Yes?" I said. "Come in." I stumbled forward into the bedroom.

Vicky opened the door. "I thought I heard someone in here as I passed down the hall." As she came toward me, she stopped. "Steven— You're ill!"

"Not exactly. A little groggy. . . . Somebody was here in the house. I surprised him here in the bedroom. He slugged me."

She swallowed with an effort. "Did you see him?"

"No. It was dark. I never got a look at him. It all happened so quickly."

She took a faltering step toward me. Suddenly she was crying. Her body shook with her weeping, and she put her arms around my waist and laid her head against my chest. Twice she said, "Oh, my God!"

She raised her face and looked at me. "You've suffered so much. I can't bear to think of it all, Steven."

"Hey," I said, "I didn't mean to upset you so much."

"I'm sorry," she said, "but I can't help it." She clung to me

as if the warmth and strength of her body could flow into mine.
Then she dropped her arms and stepped away. She didn't look
at me. "I should go now," she said.

"Why?"

"I made a fool of myself."

"No, you didn't. You're a sensitive girl. The whole thing
got under your skin for a few seconds."

"I guess it did. Can you forgive me?"

"For what? For being tender and kind?"

"I wish you weren't so damned nice," she said. She stood
there with her head hanging, biting her lip. She raised her eyes
slowly. "I'm terribly afraid for you, Steven."

"I'm not turning handsprings myself."

"He's crazy, you know," she said, her eyes meeting mine
levelly now: "the man who killed Maureen. He must be. And if
he's crazy, there's no telling what he might do."

"Don't think about such things, Vicky."

"How can I help thinking about them? He's a soul that's
damned. Can't you see, Steven? In his terrible hell, he'll strike in
any direction. He'll do anything if he fancies it will give him
relief."

"Please, Vicky . . ."

"Why do you think he came here tonight? What earthly
reason could he have?"

"I don't know."

"There's nothing here he could want. Nothing to bring
him—except one thing." She choked momentarily. "He killed
Maureen. Tonight he almost killed you. Oh, God, Steven, I'm
afraid he's trying to wipe out the whole Griffin family!"

12

She looked at me, her face pale, her eyes haggard. "I must get a grip on myself," she said at last.

"Yes." I slipped my arm around her shoulders. "Why don't you make some coffee? I've got to call Reynolds."

She nodded, and we went out of the bedroom together.

Headquarters had to reach Reynolds at home, but he showed up in a hurry. The coffee and aspirin had taken the edge off my headache by the time I opened the door at his ring.

He looked at me quickly. "Headquarters said you'd been attacked, Griffin."

"That's right," I said. I told him what had happened.

"Let's go upstairs."

We went up to the bedroom and he looked the place over. He found the razor blade near the bathroom doorway. He picked it up with tweezers that had belonged to Maureen. Light danced over the small oblong of blue steel.

"If he hadn't got the jump on me so fast," I said, "you wouldn't have to be looking for the sonofabitch. I'm going to have to be more careful, Reynolds. But if he comes back, I'm going to kill him."

"Cut out that kind of talk. You leave him to us. I'm going to have the house watched."

"You think he'll come back?"

"He didn't get whatever it was he was after. You surprised him."

"Maybe he was waiting for me."

"You said downstairs you were out all evening. He could have caught you at some more convenient spot."

"Maybe."

"Anyhow, quit talking about killing him if you get the chance."

"You're not asking me not to kill him," I said.

He wrapped the razor blade carefully in a handkerchief and put it in his side coat pocket. "You have to defend yourself."

"Thanks."

"Only, don't talk about it. I'm a cop. I don't want to hear any premeditations you might have."

He crossed the bedroom to look out of the window. He could see the trellis in the light of the corner street lamp. He closed the window. "We'll look for fingerprints and footprints, of course. Meanwhile, don't say a word about this, not even to your best friend."

"Why not?"

"You don't want to upset people, do you?"

"That isn't the reason," I said. "You're thinking that only he and I and Vicky and you know about it so far."

"You've stated it," he said. "Now I'd suggest you try to get a good night's sleep."

I was certain I wouldn't sleep. But I did. With Vicky in the spare room in case Penny woke, and a cop outside watching the house, I fell headlong into a deep pit of exhaustion the minute my head hit the pillow.

A bright sun was smiling outside my window when I awoke, but I didn't smile back.

I lay there with a bitter taste in my mouth and a sore head.

I thought of how close I'd been to him last night, and I writhed inwardly. The whole thing came flooding back to me, and I forgot how afraid I'd been of dying, how helpless after he'd hit me without warning that first time. I burned with remorse that I'd done no better. Somehow, I should have risen above myself. I could have had him.

I took a cold shower, and it helped to clear my head. I dressed and started downstairs.

I could hear them when I was halfway down the stairs. People murmuring, bringing sympathy—and its reminder of death—into the house.

I stopped on the stairway to wait a moment; when I was certain my face was composed I went into the living room.

Four people were there, all women, all friends of Maureen. I endured their condolences.

Then Willis Burke came out of the kitchen. He took in the situation and said, from the doorway, "May I see you a minute, Steve?"

I excused myself and joined Will in the kitchen.

"They mean well," he said. "They'll drift away in a few minutes." He got a cup and saucer and set them on the work area beside the sink. "You look peaked, Steve. You need some coffee. Miss Clayton left a fresh pot."

"Where is she?"

"She took Penny downtown. Too many people in and out, she said."

"I don't know what I'd have done without that girl, Will."

"She sure showed up at the right time. Must have thought the world of Maureen."

"I guess she did."

"Maureen ever mention her, or write her?"

"Not that I know of. Why?"

86

He shrugged. "Nothing. Just strange, the way she showed up."

I lowered the coffee cup from my lips. "What do you mean by that?"

"Nothing, I guess. Such coincidences do happen. Learning that Maureen had been killed—well, Vicky, being what she seems, wouldn't have had to be a close friend to have her sympathy awakened. Especially with Penny being left alone."

"That's the way I see it."

"I've got no reason to see it otherwise," Will admitted with a smile. "I guess Carla just made me grumpy this morning. She's overdrawn her personal checking account again and then had the gall to tell me I should have reminded her that she'd bought a couple of extra dresses earlier in the month."

I refilled my cup. "Will, there's a couple of business details . . ."

"Forget the business. For a month. Or for as long as necessary. The business will hobble along. Wouldn't be what it is if it hadn't been for you in the field, anyway."

"I spent too much time in the field, Will."

"I know."

"A month or two out and a weekend at home. No good."

"Take it easy, Steve."

"Even my own kid doesn't miss me. She seems quite willing to leave the house with a stranger."

"Don't forget that you introduced her to the stranger. Penny wouldn't leave with just any stranger."

"Still—" I set my cup down. "I'm feeling sorry for myself."

"I guess you are."

"It's no good."

"None whatever," he said. "What's Reynolds found out?"

"Nothing. At least, not that I know of. We went to the

nursery and supermarket yesterday. A kid at the store saw her almost get hit."

"Any identification?"

"No. Will, have you or Carla had occasion to use my car at any time in the past few weeks?"

"Why, no. Why should we use your car?"

"I don't know. Do you know of anybody she might have loaned the car to?"

"She was careful about that sort of thing, Steve, especially when you were away."

"How about Randy Price?"

"You mean the young guy who's trying to write plays?"

"Yes."

"Ease yourself on that score," Will said. "I don't know Price very well; I met him briefly. But I know how Maureen felt about him."

"And how was that?"

"Oh, she was fond of him. She believed he was loaded with talent. As a person, he was sort of like a child to her. Precocious, stimulating, somebody who needed help and protection. I doubt that she would have let him go chasing off with the car while you were out of town."

"I see."

Will rinsed his coffee cup in the sink, looking over his shoulder at me. "Steve, I think you were after something. Two attempts were made on her life with a car that's a twin to yours. Though nobody saw the third try made, it's almost certain that she was killed with the twin car."

"Something like that."

"And that could only mean that somebody struck back for something your car did."

I said, "You've reasoned it out."

"I'll reason a little further," Will went on, quietly. "You

88

were thinking she might not have been driving the car when it did whatever it was supposed to have done. You were thinking somebody might have borrowed the car."

"I didn't mean it personally, Will."

"Okay," he said. "Forget it."

We walked into the living room, and I lighted a cigarette.

"Reynolds is no genius," Will said. "But he's a tough, shrewd cop, for all his dandy looks. He's accustomed to searching for patterns. Maybe he's found one in the car, after all."

"Then you know something about it?"

"No, but I know something was bothering Maureen, as I mentioned night before last. And it didn't start when the guy first tried to run her down, either."

"You'd noticed it before?"

"Yes."

"Precisely when?"

He walked over to the window and looked out at the morning. "I think I first noticed it one afternoon about three weeks ago." He turned to face me. "I ran into her downtown. She didn't see me right away, and I was little shocked at the way she looked—like she'd lost her last friend. She was standing on the sidewalk, looking in the window of a florist's shop. The people passing about her, the noise of the city all seemed a million miles from her."

"Just standing there?"

"Just standing there."

"I don't get it."

"Neither did I," Will said. "I thought she was ill. She jumped about three feet when I spoke to her. For a second she was a long-lost little girl who'd been caught in some mischief.

"She got control of herself right away. She brightened, even managed a smile. In fact, she managed so well that I decided she was simply tired. I invited her to have a drink, but she said she had to get home, that the baby sitter's time was up, and that Penny had probably driven the poor old soul to distraction already. She was still smiling, outwardly at ease, but I had the feeling that she wanted to see me hurry on, that she wanted me to mind my own damned business.

"I made a parting bright remark. I glanced at the flower shop and, knowing there'd been no deaths in your family or hers recently, I said, 'Rich uncle kick off and you're getting some flowers for the funeral?'

"For a second I thought she was going to burst into tears. Then she pulled the wreckage of her face back together in a second and said that she wanted some flowers for the house."

"You remember the florist?"

"Sure. The little place on the corner of Second and Park."

I snubbed out my cigarette. "Reynolds asked me to come by this morning, Will."

"Can I drop you?"

"No, thanks. Stick around as long as you like."

"I'll go on down to the office. I was just hanging around until you got up to see if there was anything I could do. I'll see you later, Steve."

"Sure."

I watched Will leave the house and go out to his car, which was parked at the curb.

Then I went upstairs.

I wasn't going to see Reynolds, of course. I was going to the florist's shop. I didn't want Will tagging along. I was afraid. Afraid that I might find a closer link to the motive of a cold, cruel man who had lived only to smash her.

I borrowed a lesson from the cops.

When I left the house I had a small picture of her in my coat pocket.

13

The Blossom Shoppe was a cubbyhole business enterprise wedged between a ladies' clothing store and a cafeteria on a busy street.

I paused outside the shop and lit a cigarette. The front window was a bank of flowers. There was an emblem on the window, a figure of Mercury with winged feet, showing that the shop belonged to a telegraph delivery service. A name in gold leaf on the lower left-hand corner of the window said *Mary Dorrance, prop.*

A bell tinkled when I opened the door and stepped inside. The shop was a profusion of flowers, and their aromas had gathered in the place for so long that my sense of smell was overpowered, sweetly, almost sickeningly. A slender, small woman of middle age came out of the rear of the shop. She had misty blue eyes, gray hair, and a gentle little smile.

"May I help you?"

"Mrs. Dorrance?" I asked.

"Miss Dorrance," she corrected, keeping her soft smile. "You want some flowers for a lady, sir? Roses?" She tilted her head to study me. "You appear to me to be the rose-buying type."

"No," I said. "I want a funeral wreath."

Her smile vanished. "Please forgive me!" She moved behind

the high glass case that held baskets and sprays. "That was extremely untactful of me, but you are young and . . ." Her voice limped into silence. "A friend?"

"My wife."

"Oh, I *am* sorry."

"I don't know much about flowers," I said. "I'll leave it to you. Something nice."

"I understand."

"She was a gay and kind person. I think she'd like some color in the wreath. She wouldn't want it to be too somber."

"I'll do my very best, Mr.—"

"Griffin."

"I certainly will, Mr. Griffin. Where is the service to take place?"

"It hasn't been set yet. Nor the time. I'll call you."

"That'll be fine."

"I'll pay you now," I said.

"I can do something very nice for thirty-five dollars."

I took out my checkbook and wrote her a check. She accepted it, moved over to her small, cluttered desk, and wrote a receipt.

"I'll attend to everything, Mr. Griffin. Just call me as soon as you can."

"I'll do that," I said. I took the receipt from her, and added, "My wife was here in your shop about three weeks ago. You might recall her."

"Was she a regular customer?"

I shook my head.

"There are so many people," Miss Dorrance said, with her soft smile.

I took the small picture of Maureen from my pocket and offered it to her.

She took the picture, drew black-rimmed reading glasses from the pocket of her smock, and put them on. "So young and

92

lovely," she said. Her eyes were large and very misty behind the glasses. "I'm sorry, Mr. Griffin, I don't recall the name. The picture—"

She tilted her head, holding the picture at arm's length, then bringing it closer.

"The picture," she said at last, "does strike a memory. Someone very like her. . . . About three weeks ago, you say? I remember a face like hers. An interesting face— Of course! The nervous woman!"

"Nervous?"

"Yes, I place her now. She upset a basket beside the door and insisted on paying for it. Her hands were shaking something fierce. She was very pale. Bereaved and grief-stricken, I thought at the time. But she was ill, wasn't she? I mean, now that she's deceased, I can understand how ill she must have been."

"And you don't remember the name?"

"I'm sorry. I don't. The name—Griffin—means nothing to me."

"She might have given a different name."

The little lady handed the picture back to me.

"May I use your phone?" I asked.

"Of course. There on the desk."

She had to clear away a mound of old bills and invoices to unearth the phone. I sat down and dialed Headquarters, then asked for Homicide. But Lieutenant Reynolds was out. Probably checking auto body repair shops, I guessed.

"I want to see him right away," I said. "This is Steve Griffin. I think I have something important."

"We can radio him in."

"Send him to the florist at the corner of Second and Park. The Blossom Shoppe, it's called."

"Something concerning your wife, Mr. Griffin?"

"Yes."

"We'll have him down there in short order."

"Thanks." I hung up.

Miss Dorrance was standing close to me as I turned. Her face was pale. She took a step back as I got to my feet.

"Really, Mr. Griffin, I have no idea of what this is all about. But to call the police . . ."

"Don't misunderstand, Miss Dorrance. I—and the police—want your help."

"But what—"

"You sold some flowers," I said, "to my wife. To the nervous woman. My wife wasn't ill. She didn't die a natural death." Miss Dorrance stared. "She was killed. By a hit-and-run driver."

"Mercy!"

"There's a chance that the name she used here, the address to which she had the flowers sent, might help the police."

"I shall most certainly do all I can, in that case," Miss Dorrance said emphatically.

She opened a dusty steel filing cabinet beside the desk, pursed her lips, and touched her chin with a fingertip. Her forehead creased, as if with pain. Then she began going through the file. She was still at it when Reynolds arrived less than fifteen minutes later.

Miss Dorrance acknowledged my brief introduction—"How do you do, Lieutenant?"—without leaving her file.

"What's up, Griffin?" Reynolds said to me.

I told him of Will's chance meeting with Maureen outside the shop about three weeks ago. "She was a very nervous woman when she came in here, Miss Dorrance says. It jibes with the impression Will got of her that day. And we've never bought flowers here—only at the nursery you and I went to yesterday. I want to know three things, Reynolds: Why she let a visit to a florist upset her so much, who she bought the flowers for, and under what name."

"You don't have to draw me a picture," Reynolds said shortly.

94

Miss Dorrance called excitedly, over her shoulders, "Well, I do believe this is it!" She drew a daily sales sheet from the file. "Jane Brown. I recall thinking that it was odd, such a common, lackluster name for such a striking woman. Yes, now that I see the name again, I'm sure this was she."

Reynolds said, "Do you always put down the customer's name?"

"Oh, no. But when we sell flowers for special occasions we of course ask for the names of the sender and recipient. How else should we arrange for delivery?"

"What do you term a special occasion?"

"Wedding, big party, funeral."

"And what was this particular purchase?"

"A funeral basket. A very expensive funeral basket."

I glanced at Reynolds. I could see the heat of the scent rising in him like a fever. Bloodhound fever.

"Where'd she have you send them?" he asked.

"She didn't have them sent any place," Miss Dorrance said. "When I asked for the name, she hesitated and said Jane Brown. Then when I asked where the basket should be sent, she hesitated again and said she'd take the flowers with her. She was exceedingly impatient. She didn't want to wait until I had made up a basket. She purchased one I already had on display."

A short silence crept in under the sweet smell of the shop. Maureen had bought flowers for an unknown person's funeral. But because she'd had a dread of being traced, she had dropped a barrier across her movements and actions. And we'd run head on into it. She'd thwarted us. But not him, not the smasher in the big green sedan.

"Is there anything else you can tell us, Miss Dorrance?" Reynolds insisted. "Did she do or say the slightest thing to give you an idea of where she might be taking those flowers?"

Pursed lips. Misty eyes pinched at the corners. "No, sir," she said finally.

"You make funeral wreaths regularly," Reynolds said. "Did you make many on that particular day?"

"I can't recall. I could look it up."

"Never mind. We can check."

"I wish I could help more, Lieutenant."

"I wish you could too. She carried the basket right out with her?"

"No, sir. She said she'd get her car. I watched her go outside. She stood out there for a few moments. A man joined her, and they chatted for a short time on the sidewalk."

"That would have been Willis Burke," I told Reynolds. He nodded.

Miss Dorrance glanced at me, looked back at Reynolds. "The gentleman went on. Then Mrs. Griffin went down the street. A little later, she came back in the car, tapped the horn, and double-parked long enough for me to hurry out with the basket. I put the basket in the back seat of her car."

"She was alone all this while?"

"Yes, sir, except for that short period when she talked to the man on the sidewalk."

"You've been very kind and helpful, Miss Dorrance," Reynolds said.

She followed us to the doorway. "I'm very sorry about your wife, Mr. Griffin."

"Thank you," I said.

Reynolds and I moved down the busy sidewalk. The black car was in a loading zone in front of a store half a block away. My own was in a parking lot around the corner. We stopped beside his car. "Don't let it get you down, Griffin. It happens like this all the time."

"I thought it was a good lead."

"It was. It gave us one clue. She bought flowers for somebody's funeral and she didn't want anything to point to the fact that she had done so. There are only a limited number of reasons for a person to cover up the purchase of a funeral basket."

The invisible band, stronger than steel and more merciless, began to draw tight about my skull.

"We've got the date of purchase," Reynolds went on. "Twenty-three days ago. The flowers would have been used within two or three days at the most. So now we check funerals. Every funeral for three days beginning twenty-three days ago."

"Will you know which one it is?"

"We'll check out every detail on each of them. When we find one with an automobile as the cause of death, we may have hit the right one."

"My automobile," I said. "Driven by Maureen."

"Take it easy, Griffin. We're not sure yet."

"You are."

"It's all circumstantial so far."

"Not to him. He was so certain, he killed her. With a heavy green car."

Reynolds glanced around. Two or three people on the sidewalk had slowed, were staring at me.

"Go home and rest, Griffin," Reynolds said.

"I rested last night. I'm tired of resting." Damn him, he took the circumstantial evidence and condemned her. He didn't think that maybe he could be wrong. He didn't give her a chance to explain.

"She wasn't mean, Reynolds. She wouldn't have hit somebody and left them lying on the street!"

"In a moment of panic we can never be sure what we'll do. Now forget it. Go home. Get your mind on something else!"

I had sudden tears in my eyes. Right there on the sidewalk. I didn't care. "She hit somebody—killed somebody—then bought flowers for their funeral? Don't make me laugh!"

Reynolds said nothing. He simply looked at me with pity.

I had said it. I had outlined it: If she had hit somebody and panicked, she *was* the kind who would suffer remorse, and who might even buy a basket of flowers for the funeral!

I turned and took a couple of blind stumbling steps away.

"Griffin!"

"Yes?" I looked at Reynolds over my shoulder.

"You did the right thing. It was a good lead, and it belonged to the police. Keep doing it that way, Griffin. You're shrewd. Even cunning. You're thinking too hard about it, about him. You might run onto something else. Don't try any solo flights. You just might find him—and they lock you up for any sort of killing. Even nuts."

"I don't know what you're talking about."

"Fine," he said. "I'll keep in touch."

14

When I returned home and entered the living room, Penny met me with a rush. Her cheeks were stained with tears. She grabbed my hand. "Daddy, Mommy's not gone forever, is she? She'll come home soon, won't she, Daddy?"

Vicky stood behind the child, pain in her eyes. I picked Penny up, swung her high, and held her against me.

"My Mommy's coming back, isn't she, Daddy?" Penny begged, her voice muffled against my shoulder. Her fine-boned little body trembled as she clung to me.

"Your Mommy will always be here," I said. "Even if you don't see her, she's here right now."

"Is she?"

She raised her face to look at me, and I nodded solemnly. "People we love are never really gone, Penny. Your Mommy will always be watching over you."

"Like an angel?"

"Exactly."

"And she *will* come back?"

Vicky caught a sob in her throat.

"Penny," I said, tilting her chin with my fingers to put

our eyes on a level, "you mustn't worry your Mommy with this kind of carrying on."

"But they said . . ."

"Now, you pay no attention to what anybody says. Mommy would be upset if she knew you were worrying about her. You wouldn't want to make her feel bad, would you?"

"Oh, no, Daddy!"

I sat down with her in my arms. I let her straddle my knees. "Did you have a nice time downtown?"

"Uh-huh. Vicky and I bought some hankies."

"That's fine." I set her on the floor. "Now you run upstairs and use one of those hankies on your dolly. The poor little baby caught cold last night."

"She did?"

"Oh, just a little bit of a cold, but you'll have to nurse her."

Penny turned and ran from the room. I listened to her footsteps race overhead.

Vicky's face was pale. "Steven, Mrs. Burke and two of her friends dropped by. It was 'poor Maureen this' and 'I can't believe the dear is gone' and 'poor Maureen that.' Penny overheard enough to frighten her."

"This place isn't good for the child," I said. "Will Burke has a cottage at the lake. Penny would be better off there until after the funeral, I think." I ran my hand through my hair.

"Poor Steven," Vicky murmured. "You're very tired, aren't you?"

"Yes. I wish I could be sure what's best for Penny."

"The lake cottage should be the answer," Vicky said.

"After all you've done—could you—would you . . ."

"Of course, Steven. I'd like a day or two on a lake shore myself."

"I don't know how I can ever pay you back."

100

"Pay me back?" Vicky echoed. A tide of feeling rose in her, reached her eyes. She was unable to speak for a moment. "I'm only glad I can do something for you and Penny."

"I'll call Will and ask him for the use of the cottage. I know it'll be all right. We've been out there on weekends. Penny loves the place. I'll leave you well stocked with food and money. If you should get lonely or have something else you need to do, I can hire a governess."

"Don't worry about me, Steven."

"Is it all right with your relatives for you to be visiting here?"

"Of course. I called them this morning. They understand."

"Good," I nodded. "Then it's settled."

"And you—you'll come back here burning with the desire to find the man who did this terrible thing to Penny." Vicky's eyes searched my face. But I didn't answer, and finally she said, "You mustn't, Steven." Her voice was very low. "Feeling as you do won't bring Maureen back. It can only leave scars inside you."

I got out of my chair, lighted a cigarette, and walked over to the window. "Reynolds is on a hot scent," I said. "He thinks that Maureen killed someone, and that somebody set out to kill Maureen in revenge."

"You knew her. Could she have killed?"

"She might have accidentally, and then run in panic. But for this man, whoever he is, to plot her death and smash the life out of her . . ."

"Perhaps his mind was unhinged by grief, Steven."

I turned and looked at Vicky. Her face was white.

I asked, "Why should I forgive him? Should I say to Reynolds, 'Let's go easy on this guy—after all, he was suffering when he killed my wife'?"

"Right now," Vicky said in a choked tone, "you're in the same predicament he was, feeling the same things he must have felt."

"But he didn't forgive Maureen! He didn't give her a chance. Whatever she had done, she was going to confess. Her mind was prepared for a full confession when she called me."

"But if there is never any forgiveness, where is there any hope?" Vicky's eyes were bright with tears. "Someone has to break the chain of hatred, Steven."

"He should have thought of that," I said. I took a deep breath, crossed the room to her, and took her hands in mine. She dropped her gaze to the carpet.

"I'm sorry, Vicky. You came here to visit an old friend, found her gone, and found yourself deep in my trouble. You've done more than enough."

"Hadn't we better see about the lake cottage?" she asked dully.

I phoned Will at the office. "I know Penny's going to learn eventually," I said, "but I want her to be used to her mother being gone. I want it to come gradually. Not as a shock."

"And you're right," Will said.

"I want to send her up to your lake cottage for a few days. Until after the funeral. Until after the police and callers have stopped parading through the house."

"The cottage is yours for as long as you like, Steve. You know where the spare key is hidden under the brick behind the garage."

"Thanks, Will."

"Forget it. Wish I could do more."

Vicky, Penny, and I went to the lake in two cars. I'd rented one for Vicky to use at the cottage while she and Penny were there. They followed, while I drove my sedan. The lake was about a half-hour drive from the city.

We turned up the private, graveled road that ran from the highway. As we crested a hill, we looked down the length of a pleasant valley. The gentle hills sheltering the valley were wooded and cool, and the fields were dappled with the color of wild flowers. In the distance was the lake, blue as a piece of sky.

We drove down the narrow road to the cottage. I pulled the sedan up behind the house and Vicky parked behind me. Set on the slope of the hillside, the cottage was large and rambling, yet it gave a feeling of rustic snugness. It had a long railed porch that overlooked the lake. A hundred yards beyond the porch the wind on the lake sent little feathers of water against the pilings supporting a boathouse and wooden pier.

We got out of the cars. Penny was already excited by a noisy jay who hopped on the railing of the porch with his head cocked to one side. She laughed as the jay tried to order us away in a raucous voice.

I went around the garage, got the cottage key, came back to the sedan, and loaded my arms with groceries. Vicky unlocked the door and we entered a long living room. Overhead were hand-hewn beams. The furnishings were simple, big, comfortable. At one end of the room was a yawning fieldstone fireplace.

"Well!" Vicky said, looking the room over.

"There are two bedrooms, a bath, a dining room, and a kitchen back here." I carried the groceries to the kitchen and set them on a table. Vicky looked at the refrigerator, the freezer, the gleaming electric stove.

"I feel just like a pioneer," Vicky said.

"There's a small outboard cruiser in the boathouse. Want me to get it out for you?"

"Thanks, but my sea legs are none too steady. Anyway, Penny might fall overboard."

"I'll check the power generator before I leave."

"For that I'll give you a cup of coffee."

We had the coffee and Vicky followed me to the car. "Steven—don't let him kill you too."

"I'll be careful."

"I don't mean that," she said.

I slid behind the wheel. She was standing beside the car. "Find room in your heart for pity, Steven," she said softly.

"It's almost as if you were pleading his case."

She shook her head. "What he's done is over," she said. "It's the aftermath—its effect on you—that's what I'm thinking about. Hate is a cancer of the spirit, Steven. I don't want to see you destroyed by it. Do you understand?"

I sat with my hands on the wheel for a little while. Then I said, "I won't get over Maureen for a long time, Vicky. You know that, don't you?"

"I wouldn't respect you if you didn't feel that way about her, Steven."

"When all this is over, you'll understand your own feelings better."

"Perhaps you're right."

I started the car, then turned it around. As I drove over the crest of the hill, I looked back. She hadn't moved. She stood straight and still. The sparkling blue of the lake was the right setting for her.

15

Reynolds was parked in front of the house in the police car. I stopped the sedan in the driveway. Reynolds and I met in the yard and entered the house.

"I took Penny to the country."

He nodded. "The best thing for the kid."

He pitched his hat on a chair, then sat on the couch. "No funerals involving the victim of a hit and run," he said.

Something snapped and went limp inside me. "Then I was right. She couldn't have done such a thing."

"Maybe."

"What do you mean, maybe?" I said angrily. "You tried to find your motive in some low act she did. But you still don't know. You still don't have the reason."

"No, I don't," Reynolds admitted. "I checked every funeral for over a week, beginning twenty-three days ago. She wouldn't have bought the flowers a whole week prior to the funeral. So it looks like no dice."

"Have you thought she might have been buying the flowers for someone else?"

"A friend, someone who perpetrated a hit-run and then got her to buy the flowers?"

"Something like that."

"Then explain the car. Why'd he use the same kind of car as yours, same color?"

"He might have happened to own a twin to the sedan. Have you thought of that?"

"Pretty farfetched." For a moment, Reynolds looked tired. Seeing his eyes, and the lines in his face, I glimpsed something of the effort he had been putting into this thing. "A better explanation would be that she loaned your car."

"We've been over that."

"So we have. Then there's one thing left—whoever she hit didn't live here in town. She was out of town when it happened."

The brief moment of sympathy I'd felt for him was gone in a flash of heat. "Why are you so damned determined that she killed somebody?"

"I'm not," he said quietly, "I hope she didn't. But it's the only explanation I see."

"Have you checked repair garages, auto-body shops?"

"I've had a man on that."

"And you've found no evidence that my sedan was repaired, have you?"

"Not yet. We still have several garages to go. Some of the small ones in the suburbs." A hard look came into his eyes. "It's got to work. There has to be a garage that did the job."

"Otherwise?"

"We're up a stump. We'll have to go back and find a new tack."

"Or fail."

"We won't fail, Griffin."

"You've failed so far. You've done everything you can to make her responsible for her own murder. It hasn't worked. Why? Because she wasn't responsible."

"There has to be a reason," he said doggedly. "Something she did to cause him to run her to earth."

"Why must there be a reason?" I said. "Maybe he's a downright lunatic. Maybe he saw her on the street one day and decided to kill her. Such a thing isn't impossible, you know."

"It is in this case," Reynolds said. "Because she knew the reason and she knew the man. She knew he was trying to kill her—and why. She was ready to confess to you—and to the police as soon as you got home and could be with her."

I stood looking at Reynolds, coming close to hating him. I'd lived through the first horror of wondering if she had done something terrible. I'd just about convinced myself she hadn't.

"We'll get him," Reynolds said, "and maybe the reason won't look so bad then." He stood up and let his hand fall on my shoulder. "His crime isn't perfect. No crime is."

"How about the unsolved ones?" I said. My voice shook. They had to get him. They mustn't fail. Not only to take an eye for an eye, but to bring the reason to light, so that I could know it for what it was. She might not have been guilty after all. It was something I had to learn. I couldn't go through life with him free and the reason forever hidden from me.

"There's not one unsolved crime that isn't studded with mistakes," Reynolds insisted. "A crime in itself is a piece of folly, a foolish, illogical act, contrary to common sense and to the good of the group of which the criminal is a part. An unsolved crime means only that a dull, uninterested cop has slipped up, or that lack of money and manpower has caused available resources to be concentrated on newer crimes."

"Perfect enough from where the crook sits," I said. "There's not a thing to stop him from growing old, dying in bed, and having grandchildren honor his grave with a bouquet of posies."

Reynolds stared at me as if he were addled. Then his eyes glowed. "Of course!" he said.

"Of course what?"

"The flowers—Griffin, you've hit it!"

"What did I say?"

"Why assume the flowers were for a funeral?"

"And what else would a funeral basket be for?"

"A bouquet to honor a grave. A grave already in existence. A grave several days old. If she killed somebody with that big green sedan and then ran away, she wouldn't have gone to the funeral." He paused to take a breath. "She would have been afraid. The fear and shame would have still been too fresh, too new. She wouldn't have had time to get used to living with them. She might have been noticed, at the funeral.

"But the funeral was all over. She'd carried this thing inside her until it was driving her crazy. She had to make some kind of gesture. So she buys some flowers and steals out to the grave to leave them there. Instead of starting twenty-three days ago and working down the calendar, I should have worked up." He turned quickly and went into the hallway. I heard him telephoning.

I didn't want to think about what he'd said. I turned toward the sun-lighted window and pulled a cigarette from the crumpled package in my pocket. An express truck cruised slowly down the street outside. It slowed, stopped at the curb before the house. I saw the delivery man get out of the truck, a small, oblong package in his hands. As he started up the walk, I realized he was making a delivery here.

I opened the door before the man rang.

"Mrs. Griffin's residence?" he asked.

"I'm her husband."

"Package for her. Collect. If you'll sign here, please."

He held out a metal clipboard. I signed the slip, paid him, and he gave me a copy of the slip and the package. I closed the door on his departing back and looked at the package. It was addressed to Maureen, with the printed sticker showing a return address to Hull and Jordan, Authors' Representatives, New York City.

I ripped the package open. Its contents were two Randy Price play manuscripts and a letter on Hull and Jordan stationery.

The letter read:

"Dear Mrs. Griffin,

"Pursuant to our correspondence of a month ago, we have had both Mr. Hull and Mr. Jordan read the enclosed manuscripts.

"These plays aroused considerable interest in this office. However, while they indicate the author has promise, the scripts also unfortunately reflect immaturity and inexperience.

"The return of these efforts does not mean that we are averse to seeing more of the work of Randy Price. On the contrary, we wish to assure Mr. Price that he definitely has a storehouse of talent, if these plays are any indication. He reveals a feeling for people, and a crude but promising way of hitting home with his unique ideas about life.

"Please be assured that anything of his you care to send will receive a most sympathetic reading here. All our resources will be used to his advantage the moment he produces something that is a bit more polished and professional than the enclosed manuscripts.

"Thank you for calling the work of Mr. Price to our attention.

"Yours sincerely,
"Roger W. Hull"

There was a postscript jotted in ink, an afterthought when Hull's secretary had laid the letter on his desk for signature:

"P.S. I certainly do remember you, Maureen, from my days as an actors' agent. So now you're married and have a little girl? I know she must be as wonderful as her talented mother, and I'm sure the lucky man you married is everything a man should be. Next time I go to the Coast on a business trip I'll try to stop off to see you, meet your husband, and talk to Mr. Price. I did my stint in service since I last saw you. I began handling authors instead of actors when I donned civvies again. Your friend, RWH"

I slid the manuscripts in a table drawer, folded the letter, and put it in my pocket. I would give it to Randy Price the next time I saw him. I knew it would please him.

As Reynolds came into the room, I quit thinking of anything except the expression on his face.

"You want to go?" he said.

"Where?" I asked.

"To West End."

I nodded. We walked out of the house, got into the police car, and as Reynolds pulled away from the curb he said, "Being a cop is a nasty job, at best." Preparing me. "Somebody has to do it," he said. "Sometimes I hate being right." He looked grim.

West End. It must have happened there. What could she have been doing in that section of town?

"I'm sorry," Reynolds said, letting me know, letting me guess, feeding it to me gradually. "There is still a chance it could have been some other car."

"Quit tiptoeing, Reynolds!"

"All right," he said, looking straight ahead as he drove, "here it is. Twenty-eight days ago, at eight fifty-five in the evening, a young woman stepped from the curbing on West End Avenue."

"Go on."

"She wasn't alone," Reynolds said.

"Her husband?"

"No."

"A child?"

"She had a little boy in her arms."

I closed my eyes. I was going numb. "Which one of them?" I asked.

Reynolds didn't speak right away. Then: "Just as the woman stepped from the curb, a car swung wide at the intersection. It was moving fast, and skidded. It went out of control."

"Both of them," I said dully.

110

"Yes," Reynolds' voice was gentle.

A short, crazy laugh burst out of me. "That was Maureen. Never did anything halfway. She didn't kill one. She killed two. Mother and child. Clean sweep."

"Take it easy, Griffin."

"A woman and her little boy!" I said.

Reynolds slowed the car. "Get a grip on yourself," he said.

I heard him, and after a minute his words began to make sense. The external world swam into focus. Streets, trees, hedges, houses. An untroubled sonofabitch up ahead mowing his yard while his wife sat on the porch watching him. He stopped the mower, wiped sweat from his face with his forearm, looked at his wife. They smiled at each other, and he gave the mower a shove. Safe, contented.

"Tell me, Reynolds. Did they live long?"

"Not very long," Reynolds said. "When the car bore down on the woman and her child, she tried to throw the little boy to one side. She wasn't in time. The car couldn't stop. The woman and boy were buried two days later."

"And the car didn't stop," I said.

"Hit-run told me," Reynolds said, "that the car slowed for a moment, sluing in the street. Then it picked up speed and got out of there fast. The driver must have panicked."

"Hit-run is still looking for the car?"

"Yes," Reynolds said.

"Parked at my house. Right at this moment."

"It looks that way," Reynolds admitted. "The boys on the hit-run detail got the usual garbled, conflicting description of the car. Everything happened very quickly. No witnesses thought of getting the license number. Hit-run is certain of only one thing—the car was a heavy, dark green sedan."

We drove across the downtown area, then out through the ragged fringe of the business section.

Finally I had to ask it. "Who were they?"

"People by the name of Martin. The woman's husband owns a hole-in-the-wall grocery over on West End. We'll learn more about him. Bill Ravenel is meeting us. He's been on the case."

16

At the turn of the century, West End had been an address of distinction. Genteel quiet had reigned over large, impressive gingerbread houses. Fine carriages reposed in the carriage houses or were pulled along the street by matched teams. Proper good mornings were exchanged on a sidewalk dappled by sunlight under the shade of maple trees. That world had gone with two wars, rockets, jet planes, and atomic power. Now only the ghost of the old West End remained in the hulking, gloomy houses, soured from the stale smells of cooking and inefficient sanitation.

At this hour of the afternoon, West End was filling with people pouring from the industrial edge of the city into the ghost houses that had been chopped into crowded apartments. Only a few of the old maple trees remained, and these were ragged and scarred. Laundries, fixit shops, pawnbrokers, garages, cheap movies, and dives were wedged between the houses.

Reynolds parked near a corner, and a few moments later a police car swung in ahead of us. A man got out and walked back to us.

"Bill Ravenel," Reynolds said.

"How do you do?" Ravenel said curtly.

I reached across Reynolds to shake hands through the open

window of the car. Ravenel was young and tall with a boyish face
and crew cut. His blue eyes were cold. He made the handshake
short.

"Too bad about your wife, Griffin," Ravenel said.

Reynolds and I got out of the car and joined him on the
sidewalk.

"The Martins were a fine family," Ravenel said. "Life here
in West End is tough. It does one of two things to the people
who are born here. It warps them, or they—like the Martins—rise
above it. You got to be a first-class citizen to be forced to live on
West End and yet not sink to living in it. I hope it wasn't your
wife driving the car."

"Ravenel . . ." Reynolds said in a curt tone.

"Sorry," Ravenel said. His gaze held on my face and again
he said, "Sorry," his tone a little different.

He turned, and Reynolds and I followed him a few paces
down the sidewalk. Hurrying people brushed by us. Loungers in
doorways watched us. Ravenel stopped at the edge of the sidewalk
and pointed to a spot a few feet from the curbing.

"It happened there," he said.

I looked at the street blindly.

"Mrs. Martin stepped into the street," Ravenel said. "The
car came around this intersection. It was over in a second—and
the car was gone."

I closed my eyes.

"Come on," Ravenel said.

We moved on to the intersection, crossed the street, and
went down the sidewalk a dozen yards. Ravenel turned into a walk
that led to a glowering old three-story house. The yard on either
side of the cracked cement of the walk had been trampled over
the years to the hardness of a brick.

We stepped up onto the long porch that rambled across
the front of the house and down one side. In the downstairs hallway two small girls were playing jacks. Their solemn, dirty faces

114

gave us a brief moment of attention. As we started up the stairway, the faintly damp and aged smell of the house closed over us like musk. A dim bulb gave faint illumination to the rear of the second-floor hallway. A baby was crying thinly somewhere on the third floor.

Ravenel paused before a door and said, "Griffin, you're going to meet the Chevoks, Sally Martin's parents. Do you feel up to it?"

"I'll meet them," I said.

Ravenel knocked on the door. After several seconds the door swung open, framing a gaunt old man. He squinted into the dimness of the hallway. He seemed to be of middle-European ancestry.

"Oh," he said, "it's the police again."

"How are you, Mr. Chevok?" Ravenel asked.

"How should I be? I'm living," the old man said; "I'm living." He opened the door wide, stepped aside, and we entered the apartment.

The living room was furnished with an old overstuffed set of furniture. It was a heavy, crowded room, an old folks' room. But, though it gave the feeling of being cramped, it was clean and reasonably tidy.

Ravenel said, "Mr. Chevok, this is Mr. Griffin and Mr. Reynolds."

The old man nodded, shook hands with us, and raised his voice to call, "Mama."

An old lady came into the room. In her gauntness, she looked a great deal like her husband. Her face was very wrinkled, and showed little expression. She appeared to be a woman who had worked hard for many years, and who had developed a great capacity for endurance.

Mr. Chevok introduced us, and his wife asked us to sit down.

"Something new has come up?" the old man asked.

"We've got a new lead," Ravenel said. "We're not certain yet how good it will prove to be."

"You haven't found Alec yet," the old lady stated.

Ravenel shook his head. "Your son-in-law is still missing. We're doing everything possible to find him."

Neither of the old people said anything.

"These men," Ravenel said, indicating Reynolds and me, "know nothing of your son-in-law. I wish you'd tell them something of Alec, Mr. Chevok."

"What's to tell?" the old man said. He took a weary breath. "I knew him from the time he was a boy. He was a good boy. I knew him long before he married Sally. He lived with his mother and sister after his father was killed. He worked and helped his folks. He always worked. His sister was a pretty girl. She worked and got some schooling. She left the neighborhood a long time ago. Alec planned to leave too. Him and Sally, they wanted to leave."

"You told me he'd been in the army," Ravenel said.

"Yeah," the old man answered. "That was before him and Sally got married. He was in the fighting over in Korea. Alec had guts, but not the heart for killing. He nearly went crazy. His mother died while he was over there. His sister came back to West End to be with him for a while after he got home. He was all right when he got back. He could talk about Korea, and he looked to the future."

"He and Sally were married then?" Ravenel guided the old man.

"Yeah, right after he got home, him and Sally was married. It was the natural thing. Everybody figured it would happen. They lived right down the street. Alec had saved a little money. He paid down on a grocery store. It's the one on the corner.

"They was doing pretty good. Sally had the baby. Alec had to put a lot of hours in the store, but he was making it pay. They planned to move. They wanted a one-family house. Alec found a place on the edge of town. They went out there to see it the day

116

that car—that damned murdering car—" The old man gripped the arms of his chair. A vein became visible, throbbing diagonally across his forehead. The old lady folded her hands in her lap. The big hard knuckles were white.

"Sally was full of talk of the house that night," the old man said. "Alec was staying open late, and Sally and the boy were going to meet him. She got through telling Mama and me about the house, and left here laughing with the little boy and telling him what a fine place they was going to have.

"Alec was looking for them. He knew she'd come down here to tell us about the house. He was standing in the doorway of the store. Him and Sally was going to get something to eat, kind of celebrate. They waved at each other, and her and the boy started across the street. Then that big car came around the corner."

For a little while, the old man's breathing was the only sound in the apartment. His nostrils swelled and shrank with his breathing.

Ravenel started to say something. The old man said: "That's all right. I can talk about it. It nearly killed Alec. Nearly drove him crazy." He looked at Reynolds and me. Ravenel had heard the story before.

"Alec wouldn't sleep or eat," the old man said. "A man can't live without both. All he wanted to do was sit in their apartment—in the dark. Wouldn't turn on a light. I had to guide him like a blind man at the funeral.

"Me and Mama and his friends tried to talk him out of it. It didn't do any good. His sister came back to town, but she couldn't seem to help him either. Then one day—just about a week ago—Alec came here. He looked terrible. He was skin and bone. His eyes had a burning look to them. He said he couldn't stand to live on West End any longer. He was going away. He said he'd write and let us know where he was, but we haven't heard a thing from him from that day to this."

117

"So you still have no idea where he might have gone?" Ravenel asked.

Chevok turned his head slowly and looked at Ravenel. "No," he said. "He just sold the store—almost gave it away—and disappeared."

Ravenel stood up, his gaze resting on the old man. "We'll try not to bother you again."

"It's all right," the old man said heavily.

Reynolds and I rose. With Ravenel, we moved toward the door. The old man got up to open it for us.

"If you hear from him," Ravenel said, "let us know."

"All right," the old man said.

"No matter where he is. No matter what his condition. It's to his best interest that we contact him as quickly as we can."

"I'll call you," Chevok said.

We told the old couple goodbye, and Chevok closed the apartment door behind us. I followed the policemen down the gloomy stairway, through the dim, sour hall, out to the noise and grime of West End.

On the sidewalk, I stopped. "Ravenel."

"Yes?" He and Reynolds flanked me.

"Thanks," I said.

"For what?"

"For not telling them the whole of it right away. Who I am. How I might be concerned with their daughter's death, and the boy's . . ."

"I was thinking of them, Griffin, not you."

"I know. And that's right. I was thinking of them too. I'm sorry it happened. I'm more than sorry that it happened to people like that. Tell them the rest of it—the aftermath I've had to face and endure—as gently as possible."

I felt Ravenel's hand on my shoulder. His eyes had lost their hardness. "I'll do that, Griffin."

118

17

We walked up the street to the police car Reynolds had brought to West End. Ravenel sat in the back.

"Sally Chevok Martin and the kid were buried in Memorial Park," Ravenel said.

Reynolds started the car. We joined the stream of traffic and drove out of West End and across town. None of us talked much during the drive. Reynolds turned down a quiet tree-shaded street. We rode a few blocks farther and reached the white stone pillars marking the entrance to the cemetery. The gravel of the driveway crunched beneath the wheels.

"This is the one," Ravenel said.

We got out of the car. A narrow, white-graveled path led straight up the gentle grass-carpeted slope to where a small marker designated the graves of Sally Martin and her son.

At the head of the graves stood a weathered floral basket. The sod had settled a little, causing the basket to lean to one side. Clayey mud had splashed the bottom of the basket during the recent rain. The flowers had withered to dried brown pods and brittle stems.

Ravenel stepped carefully around the graves and picked up

the basket. He tapped it against the heel of his shoe to knock some mud from it, upended it, and motioned to me.

I moved up beside him. Weather had almost obliterated the sticker on the bottom of the basket. Almost. But I could still read it: *The Blossom Shoppe.*

"This is where she brought the basket," Ravenel said.

A final bleak and despairing disbelief rose in me. I knew Maureen too well. She wouldn't have killed and run, no matter what they said. I remembered her trotting alongside the stretcher in Korea. She would have stopped, tried to help.

She *couldn't* have been driving the car that destroyed the Martin family.

"It all fits too well," Ravenel said gently, replacing the basket. "She hit them. She ran. But she was tortured to the point where she had to make some gesture. So she bought the basket and brought it here herself. Martin wasn't after her right away, remember. She didn't know he would try to kill her for what she'd done. She wasn't afraid yet—not as she became later—only filled with remorse. Martin was still sitting in that dark apartment, hearing his wife's laughter and his child's footsteps in his brain.

"We can picture the rest of it. Martin lied when he said he didn't get the license number of the car. The insane desire to get revenge was in him from the very first moment. While he sat in that apartment, he plotted and fed on the knowledge that the person who did it must be suffering. He had to be lying about the license number. He was standing right in the doorway of his store. He saw the tragedy coming. He knew it was happening. He stared at the fleeing car. Believe me, he got the license number. And then he went over to the Bureau of Registration, finally, and found out who owned the car.

"Next, he must have visited your neighborhood, watched the house. He saw the car. Saw her—the woman who'd been driving it that day. He'd sold his grocery store by that time. And I'll lay you five to one he went out and paid cash for a twin of your car, Griffin—the revenge weapon."

His words crashed into my mind. I could feel the shattering impact of them down to my fingertips. "You'd better find this Alec Martin before I do," I said.

"Lay off that, Griffin."

"Martin had no business taking the law into his own hands. If he had found her, and identified her, he could have called the police."

"You'd better remember that."

"I'm not hunting a woman, Ravenel. A woman who killed by accident and then suffered for it, suffered as only a person of Maureen's decency could have suffered. I want to find a man—one who deliberately committed a crime—not accidentally. That makes a lot of difference."

"Not to me," Ravenel said. "I'll trump up a charge and lock you up if you make one phony move."

"Just find him before I do," I told him, "or you'll have a real charge."

Later, sitting in the silence of my own house, I kept thinking of the old couple we'd talked to this morning. I kept seeing a car coming around the intersection into West End.

I hurried out of the house, drove to the mortuary, made the arrangements, and escaped the hushed, artificial air of the place. The funeral would be held in two days.

I went back to the house and had dinner out of a can. I didn't bother to clean up the kitchen. In the living room, I slouched down on the couch. Nothing about the house seemed real. I closed my eyes, but I couldn't close my mind.

After a while, I sat up. It was dark outside. Dark—as it had been outside Alec Martin's apartment when he hadn't bothered to turn on a light. My forehead filmed with a fine sweat. I got up and turned on a light. I smoked a cigarette. Turned on the

TV set. Turned it off again. Finally, I went into the hall alcove and picked up the phone. I dialed the Burke number.

Will answered. "Glad you called, Steve. Carla and I were just getting ready to come over. Knew you'd be alone in the house now, with Penny and Vicky at the lake. Say, why don't you come on over here? Spend the night. I would, in your shoes. I wouldn't like to stay there alone tonight."

"I'll come over," I said.

"I'll put the coffeepot on. Or would you rather have a drink?"

"A drink. About half a pint of bourbon in a water tumbler."

Will and Carla cushioned the evening. Carla was on her best behavior, not criticizing Will once. We chatted about inconsequential things. Carla could be a charming hostess when she tried. Seeing her and Will together this way, I realized how well suited they were to each other. They stooped to inane quarreling and Carla nagged only because they were bored. The same was true of Will's benders. Against their background, and in the midst of their secure world, they hadn't had to cope with any sizable challenge from life.

Will had often expressed the view that his house was sterile, lacking in human warmth. At such times he complained that he'd envied my house, my home. So many words. Griping gave him something to do, something to take his mind from himself, a brief flight from an existence so insulated that it stifled him.

I went to bed in the guest room.

I awoke the next morning refreshed. After breakfast and heartfelt thanks to Will and Carla, I went home. Will had insisted that I forget the office for a few days.

I took the milk and morning paper inside the house. I even whistled a little as I cleaned and straightened up. It broke the silence.

122

I called the lake cottage. Vicky said that everything was fine, and that Penny was minnow fishing from the shore with a string and bent pin.

Next I called Reynolds. His news was anticlimactic. He gave it to me as if he were reading from a report. A clerk in the license bureau remembered that a man of Alec Martin's description had asked about a license-plate number. A used-car dealer recalled the sale of a big green sedan a week ago. The buyer, again, answered Martin's description. Martin's moody manner and his insistence on a certain type of car, body style, and color had caused the dealer to remember him.

"Martin checked out the license number of the car," Reynolds said. "Your car, Griffin. If he saw the license number, he must have seen whether a man or woman were driving. He pegged Mrs. Griffin as his mark. Then he bought himself a big car just like yours—and that's it. Just as we surmised."

"Now you've got to find Martin," I said.

"We'll find him. Driving a car like that one, he won't escape detection long. Relax now, Griffin. All the odds are stacked against him. The case is practically closed."

I hung up and stood in the alcove a moment longer. They would find Alec Martin, but he wouldn't die for his crime. They'd lock him up in a state institution, give him the best of medical care, food and lodging. I'd help pay for that. The taxes on property Maureen and I had worked and sacrificed to accumulate would help pay for it.

There should be another way of dealing with a man like Martin. He'd been sane enough to plan it all. And he had deliberately, viciously, committed murder. He shouldn't be excused for that.

Someone knocked on the front door. It was Randy Price. Today a secondhand blue suit was draped on his thin, wiry frame.

"Hi, Steve," he said glumly.

"Hello, Randy. Come in."

He sat down wearily in a club chair. "I had to see somebody, talk to someone. I can't work."

"That's too bad."

"I'm haunted, Steve."

"Haunted?"

"Yes," he said softly, his face white. "She gave me all the encouragement I knew. Now that she's gone—what if I can never work again?"

I didn't know what to say to that.

His gaze was fierce on my face. "Steve—I'd die without my work."

He meant it. His quiet tone gave me a shock. "You shouldn't talk like that. Maureen wouldn't like that kind of talk if she were here."

"No, she wouldn't, would she? No matter what, she'd tell me that life is short, art long."

"An apt quotation."

"I'll always remember it, Steve."

"How about some coffee?"

"Sure, if you haven't got a beer."

"We'll see. I'm afraid, though, it'll have to be coffee."

We walked back to the kitchen.

"I'm sure I'll be able to get back to work when this is over," he said.

"Of course you will."

"When they nail the guy who did it to her," he said.

"They've identified him."

"No!"

"A man named Alec Martin. Maureen ever mention him to you?"

He shook his head, his eyes tight on my face.

"It seems," I said, "that Maureen accidentally struck this Martin's wife and child with the car. Then she fled in panic. Martin got the license number and took the law into his own hands."

Randy stood before me, rubbing his Vandyke with the back of his hand. He didn't seem boyish then. He reminded me somehow of a coiled whip. I saw the same quality in him that Reynolds had spotted.

"They get this Alec Martin?" he asked softly.

"Not yet. They're looking."

"They may be looking forever, Steve. And when they find him, he won't get what he deserves."

"I realize that, too."

We stood looking at each other grimly. I began to understand. And I knew he was beginning to understand. Knowledge grew rapidly between us, like a fungus in some dark wet corner of a jungle.

"This Martin," I said. "He lived on West End Avenue. Dressed as you were when Reynolds and I called on you, you wouldn't attract much attention over there. You could ask questions. You could drift into places. You could overhear talk."

"While the police couldn't," he said.

"The police would hit a solid wall of silence on West End," I said. "So would I."

"Sure," he said. "Maureen was the Lady Gotrocks from uptown, coming among them to kill, while Alec Martin is one of them."

"You've got it," I said.

"And if I locate this Martin, and need help?"

I didn't say anything. I didn't need to.

From the front door, I watched him stride to his car. The

sun burnished his crew cut, glistening as it might on the hood of a cobra. But if he found Martin, I would have to do the rest of it. He'd made that clear.

I watched him drive away in his erstwhile taxicab. The wise hunter, I thought, against the mountain lion releases his most vicious dog.

18

I knew it was wrong.

Randy Price was near enough to genius to have a great chance of success. He was an actor. He could pose, and could gain the confidence of people. He was also cunning. He could beat the police to Alec Martin if anybody could.

It was what I wanted. It was wrong—but I wanted it. The place and time would determine a lot of things; they would dictate my actions from the moment I heard from Randy. I didn't intend to leave a trail as Maureen and Martin had.

The phone rang.

It was Will Burke. "Steve," he said, "a special delivery letter just came here to the office for you."

"Who's it from?"

"I don't know. There's no return address. Want me to open it?"

I thought for a moment. Then: "Go ahead."

I heard the faint sound of ripping paper as he held the phone and opened the letter at the same time. I could hear him breathing. But he didn't say anything.

I spoke his name twice. The third time I almost shouted it. "Will! What is it? Read me the letter!"

"It isn't a letter, Steve. It's a single typewritten line on a piece of white paper. No identifying marks or anything . . ."

"Well, tell me what it says!"

"It says: 'You owe me the kid too, Griffin.' "

It was my turn to stand silent while I held the phone.

"Steve—did you—"

"Yes, I heard you. Get Reynolds. No, I'll get him. Hang onto that note, Will."

"I'll get out to the lake," he said.

"All right— No, you mustn't do that! He may not know where Penny is. He might be watching the office, planning to follow if you or I rush out there. You might lead him right to her, Will."

"I wish there was something—"

"If there is, I'll let you know." I hung up. My sweat-wet collar was choking me. My hands were shaking so badly I misdialed once and had to try again.

I listened to Reynolds' phone buzz. Once. Twice. Three times.

Reynolds, you've got to be there. . . . You've got to be . . .

"Reynolds speaking."

"Steve Griffin," I said.

"What's happened?"

"He's after Penny."

"How do you know?"

"A note. He sent it special delivery to my office today. He says I owe him the kid too. You know Lake Apopka?"

"Yes."

"Penny's still out there, at Will Burke's cottage. I sent her with Miss Clayton. It's the cottage at the very head of the lake. Get a man out there, will you?"

128

"It's as good as done. Hold yourself together, Griffin. Are you at the office?"

"No, at home."

"I'm on my way."

I hung up and stood perfectly still. I'd been afraid before. Overseas, I'd been afraid. I'd been more than afraid when Maureen's phone call had brought me through a hundred miles of rainy night. But this fear was beyond fear.

Killing him now wouldn't be a pleasure. It would be simple necessity. He had to be found and stopped before he got to Penny. There was no alternative.

Find him soon, Randy. Get on his trail fast.

I went upstairs and opened the top drawer in the chest in the master bedroom. Up high, beyond Penny's reach, was the gun I'd brought home when I decided to go on the road.

Maureen had laughed. "I don't know which I'd fear most, the gun or a prowler."

I checked the gun. It was a snub-nosed revolver. It was loaded. I slipped it in my inner coat pocket. When Reynolds arrived, I had myself under control.

"You got his note with you?" Reynolds asked.

"No," I said as we left the house. "It's still at the office. Will Burke read it to me over the phone."

"We'll pick it up and check it later." Reynolds went around the car and got under the wheel. "It'll probably be on dime-store stationery. He wouldn't use anything to give us a lead as to where he bought the paper or the section of town he might be staying in."

As we started, he said: "Ravenel's already gone to the lake. He left as soon as we got your call. We consolidated the Martin case and the Griffin case, and Ravenel and I are working together."

Penny saw us arrive and came from the lake shore at a run.

She jumped in my arms, and I held her so tightly she winced. She wriggled to the ground, telling me what fun she was having, and I walked back with her to see the tiny fish she'd caught. I baited her pin-hook and left her at the water's edge. Then I went up the cleared slope toward the cottage. Reynolds had gone ahead.

Ravenel was sitting on the peeled log railing of the porch smoking a cigarette and looking at Vicky. She sat in a rawhide and rattan chair, body pressed back, her face pale, her eyes large. Her lips trembled when I stepped up on the porch and looked at her.

"Nothing out of the ordinary out here," Ravenel said, "except her."

"What do you mean?"

"Hell, she's Alec Martin's sister," Ravenel said. "I met her in his apartment one evening right after his wife and kid were killed."

Vicky came to her feet slowly. "What he says is true, Steven—but don't judge me before you hear what I have to say."

"Does your brother know where you are?" I asked.

"No."

"Do you know where he is?"

"I'd have told them if I did. Honestly, I would have. Do you believe me?"

"I don't know," I said. "I don't know what to think."

"Will you listen to me before you judge me?"

"Go ahead."

"I had a letter from Alec," she said. "It was an incoherent account of the tragedy that had befallen his family. It was written several days after he'd buried his wife and child. When I got to him, he was in a state of acute mental distress. He would sit in his apartment, alone, for hours. Then he would go out without saying where he was going or when he would be back." Her voice broke.

130

"I might have suspected," I said. "You never told me any-thing specific about Maureen or your friendship. And you defended Martin, begged me to forgive him: 'If there is never any forgive-ness,'" I reminded her, "'where is there any hope?'"

Her head moved from side to side. "Defended him—no, Steven. Pleaded for him, yes. And for you. Knowing that if you never forgave him your whole future would be in ruins."

"When did you last see him?" Reynolds asked.

She turned her head to look at him. "Right after he sold the store. Alec said he was going away for a while, to forget every-thing. I hoped he was snapping out of it. I helped him pack a few things in his apartment that had to be stored. There were some notes he'd made: Maureen's name and address—brief bits of information about her—a license-plate number."

"Shadowing her," Ravenel said, "when he was out of the apartment. Stalking her."

A visible shiver possessed Vicky. "He was very cunning, dealing with me," she said in a low voice. "I was making plans to go home when I saw the news in the paper. The name—Maureen Griffin. Her picture. Hit and run. I tried to tell myself it couldn't be the same woman. But rationalization wouldn't satisfy me. I went to her neighborhood—Meade Park. It was easy to pick up general information about her. I stopped in the corner drugstore, and all I had to do was buy a coke and listen. Everybody was talking about her, what had happened to her, and what it would mean to her husband and little girl."

Vicky bit hard on her lower lip and sank back in her chair. "When I learned she had a child— Well, Alec had had a child too. Alec's wife and child were both gone, but the Griffin child was still living. I couldn't bear to think of the implication."

"Right then you should have come to the police," Reynolds said.

"He was my brother," she said sadly. "Perhaps I was a fool.

I had no proof that he'd killed Maureen Griffin. I still can't believe it. If you'd known him, you'd have seen his gentleness. You'd realize that in a moment of inner agony he might think of such a thing, even plot it—but that the actual killing would have been impossible for him, unless he had gone completely mad."

Completely mad. You owe me the kid too, Griffin.

"If he were innocent," Vicky said, "and I caused his arrest, I was afraid it would finish what the tragedy had begun. But if he were guilty, I—I was afraid he might try to get to the child."

"And so, Miss Martin," Reynolds said, "you decided to assume the responsibility for the protection of the child. Is that what was in your mind when you knocked at the door of the Griffin home and introduced yourself as a friend of Mrs. Griffin?"

"I didn't believe in Alec's guilt," Vicky said. Her eyes darkened, deepened. "But if I were wrong—if he'd tried anything —I would have killed him before seeing him take another step along such a course."

"If she had wanted to harm Penny," I said, "she had ample opportunity."

Ravenel glanced at me, and nodded.

"That's true enough," Reynolds said.

"Vicky, will you stay?" I asked. "Until we find him?"

She nodded. "Thank you," she said simply.

I knew she would watch over Penny night and day.

132

19

Reynolds looked toward the lake where Penny was trailing her fishing line in the water; then he glanced over the clearing about the cottage. "This is our best natural defensive terrain," he said. "A hit-run killing couldn't be arranged, and a stranger can't come within a quarter of a mile of the place without being seen. Wherever we might try to hide the child in the city, there'd be risks. Any face in a crowd might be his, any footfall on a fire escape or in a corridor.

"I'll keep three shifts of armed men out here until we can run him to earth. I think we can guarantee the safety of the child that way, Griffin."

Reynolds phoned Headquarters, and we stayed at the cottage until the arrival of two big, capable-looking cops in plain clothes.

Reynolds gave them their instructions tersely. "You're not to disturb the child, but interest her, gain her friendship. You've kids of your own. You know how to do it. You're both friends of Willis Burke's, out here for some fishing and loafing. But don't let her out of your sight. You're her shield—and if a hair on her head is harmed . . ." He didn't finish, but both policemen nodded, and looked solemn.

Reynolds and I walked toward his car, Vicky with us. At the car I lagged, letting Reynolds get in. I looked at the honest loveliness of Vicky's face. "Those men are important," I said. "They'll protect the physical Penny. But that isn't enough."

She nodded without speaking. She understood. Our hands touched briefly. We stood a moment; then I turned and got in the car.

Reynolds drove rapidly back to town.

"It's a question of waiting now," he said. "Martin can't win. We just hold tight until the dragnet pulls him in."

Unless Randy Price found him first.

I got out of the car at the house. As I closed the car door, I said: "I may go up to the lake myself tonight. If you try to reach me for anything, and I'm not here, try the number there."

Reynolds nodded. "I'll let you know the minute we hear anything."

I watched him drive away, and then walked slowly into the house.

I was tired. I stretched out on the living-room couch, dropped my arm over my eyes, and lay there for a short time. Then I went to the kitchen and made some very strong coffee. I drank it and went upstairs to pack a bag with a few things to take up to the lake. After I had done so, I came downstairs and began to lock up the house. The phone rang. I went into the hall and answered it.

"Griffin?"

"Yes."

"This is Reynolds."

"I recognize the voice. What is it? What's happened?"

"We're pulling in the men from the lake cottage, Griffin. It's all over."

"Martin—"

"We've found him."

134

My knees went weak. I had to sit down in the small chair beside the phone stand.

"What does he say?" I asked.

"Nothing."

"Nothing?"

"He's dead."

"Dead?"

"In the river. Stone-cold and soaking-wet dead. He was in his big green weapon, sitting there on the bottom of the river."

"Reynolds, wait a minute—I've got to take this a little at a time."

He gave a short laugh. Strain had melted from him. "Okay. One thing at a time. Here it is. There's a wharf on Timmons Street, near the spot where Maureen was killed, belonging to Kukolovitch and Sons. The wharf is low and old, with a ramp to the driveway so that trucks can load and unload. Follow me?"

"Yes," I breathed.

"Martin drove right off the end of the dock, Griffin. The spot must have haunted him. He must have gone back to look at the place where he'd killed Maureen. And then, on impulse, he turned into the alley and slammed the car right off into the river. He must have done it at night. No one saw it."

"How did you find him?"

"Some teen-age boys found him," Reynolds said. "They were spearfishing from the end of the dock, diving with water goggles on. One of them took a deep dive—and there, in the depths below him, was the shadowy outline of a car. Martin's weapon—with Martin in it."

I pictured every detailed of it: The boy diving. The lurch of his heart as he looked down into the murky water and saw the car. His arrow-straight flight up through the water and into the shafting rays of sunlight, his head breaking the surface; his shouts to the other boys on the pier.

There was only one detail wrong with the picture.

"Reynolds," I said, "how about the barge that was tied up to the end of the dock?"

Reynolds asked, "What barge?"

"I was down there the morning after Maureen was killed," I said. "Seamen were docking a barge. I remember the name of the place because it was peculiar and because I saw the tugboat pulling out into midstream.

"The barge was to be loaded from Kukolovitch and Sons' warehouse. Now if kids are in the habit of fishing or swimming from the dock and the car wasn't discovered until this afternoon . . ."

"You don't have to draw me a map," Reynolds snapped. "Wait. I'll call you back."

I sat perfectly still while the minutes ticked away.

The phone rang. I grabbed it.

Reynolds said excitedly: "You're right, Griffin! The barge was there from the morning after her death until today. Martin's car had to be under it the whole time!"

"Then he drove the car off the pier the same night Maureen was killed!"

"He must have."

An icy calm crept up my limbs, into my brain. "Then there were two men," I said. "Not one. Two."

"Two?"

"Martin," I said. "He was one man. But there had to be another. There had to be a man in the car with Maureen the night Martin's wife and kid were killed. Nothing fits or makes sense if Alec Martin and Maureen were the only ones involved. But a second man explains everything—a second man who wouldn't let her stop at the scene of the accident."

"But we don't have any witnesses who saw a man in the

136

car with her the night Martin's wife and child were killed, Griffin."

"Martin saw him," I said. "He must have. He saw enough to know a woman and a man were in the car. If he saw the license number of the car, he would have seen that too."

"Then the man who was in the car with her was the man who wrote the note threatening Penny," Reynolds said.

"Right. Somebody thought he was being real smart, writing that note. He thought he had a good reason for writing it. The car—Martin's car—hadn't been found, and the man who put the car—and Martin—in the river began to breathe again, began to believe that the water was deep enough so that the car would never be found. The note clinched the case against Martin. With the police running in circles, not knowing the man they were trying to find was buried deep in the river, the man who wrote the note was perfectly safe. Or so he thought. Only he didn't know about the barge—and he didn't realize what it does to a man to have the life smashed out of his wife!"

"Listen, Griffin, if you know anything—"

"I'll see you around."

"Griffin!"

I hung up. Seconds later I was driving away from the house.

The man.

He sat perfectly still in the quiet room, and the last red rays of the sinking sun came through a window at my back and struck him full in the face. He didn't blink. He looked at the gun in my hand and he listened to me talk.

"This guy Martin," I said. "A decent, gentle guy. He sees his wife and kid get killed and he gets a license number and he knows the name of the woman who was driving the car. Maureen Griffin. He plans to kill her. He wants to kill her, wants it more than anything. And he wants to know the identity of the man who was with her that night. He kills her a thousand times over in his mind—and yet, after making two attempts, once at a nursery and again at a supermarket, he fails.

"Why? Because he wasn't made of the stuff of which killers are made. Because something deep in his character caused him to fail each time. The boy at the supermarket said the car swerved away from Maureen at the final instant.

"Does Martin wait and try a third time? No. After his failure at the supermarket he must have realized he couldn't do it—not that way. Instead of stalking Maureen like a hunter, which he isn't, Martin goes to the house. He's there long enough to smoke a cigarette and leave the stub in an ash tray.

"He had her dead to rights, and Maureen knew it. Maybe she was glad of it, thankful that it was over, glad that she could face the thing at last. But she doesn't fully realize the desperation of the second man, the man who was with her the night of the hit-run accident, the man who had arrived at her house before Martin did!

"I can pinpoint the time of this man's arrival. She was phoning me. She had kept it to herself as long as she could. She told me she was in danger, and she would have told me more, but she cut the call short with a plea for me to hurry. I've wondered why she didn't tell it all to me on the phone. There's only one answer. Somebody arrived at the house, the man who was with her the night the Martin woman and child were killed. It just wasn't like her to run from a thing like that, to hide—unless somebody was working hard to make her keep quiet.

"So she talks to this man, knowing that I'm on the way. She tries to stall him until help arrives. But Martin arrives sooner.

"The man is a little too tough for Martin. He knocks him out and dumps Martin in Martin's own car. He slugs Maureen and forces her to go with him. He heads for Timmons Street for one reason. He knows he must write 'finish' to this thing for good.

138

He realizes now that Maureen is as great a danger as Martin. Her next action will be to go to the police. He must kill Martin. He knows that. And, once a man lets his mind sink to the acceptance of murder, a second killing isn't hard to think about—especially if it will wrap up the whole thing in a neat package and leave him forever safe.

"The man looks over Timmons Street and confirms his choice. The street is dark, deserted. There is no one to see, and the river is close by. He throws Maureen out of the car. She is dazed from his slugging, an easy target as he backs the car, throws it in gear, and gives it the gas.

"Then he runs Martin's car off the end of the dock with Martin in it.

"Duck soup. Nobody will ever know. He thinks he will remain free to the end of his self-centered life. No prison for him . . . Murders have been committed for less pressing motives.

"How does it read, Randy? Like a play?"

Price moved then. He stood up, and smiled contemptuously; but his eyes were hard as agate stones as he faced me in his lonely shack.

20

"It would make a lousy play, Steve. Surely you're not insinuating that I'm this mysterious and criminally brilliant man?"

"I *know* you are. You were lucky, but you made several small mistakes. You were a little too worried. For one thing, even after Martin and Maureen were gone, you were afraid she might have left something behind to connect you with the whole thing. You knew the generous impulsiveness of her character. The more you thought it over, the more urgent became the question. Had she saved news clippings about the hit-run, written anything in a diary, left anything else that might arouse suspicion? You had to look through her things.

"It was you who attacked me in the bedroom when I interrupted your search. It had to be a strong, wiry, agile, athletic man to do what you did and get out as you did when Penny and Vicky returned to the house."

"Did you see who did it?"

"No, but that doesn't matter, in the light of other things. The note, for example, threatening Penny. Neither Reynolds nor I had broadcast it that the police had pinned Alec Martin as the man wanted for Maureen's death. But I told you, and you put on an act, and went out and, in the light of what you'd learned, wrote the note. You posted it special delivery; the time element dovetails perfectly. A special delivery posted right after our talk would have been delivered here in the city at the time the note hit my office. It was clever to address it to the office, but it wasn't strong enough to serve as a smoke screen, Randy.

"You wrote the note without knowing that a barge was at the dock, floating above the car, and that Martin had remained among the missing for that reason. You naturally thought that, if he hadn't been found in the time that had elapsed, he wouldn't perhaps ever be found, and you wanted the whole case closed, with the police believing that Martin had killed Maureen.

"The removal of the barge and the finding of Martin's body diverted suspicion from Martin. The note, which had been a brilliant stroke, backfired and became a dumb move. For when the note failed to point at Martin, it pointed directly at you, Randy. The note—and the little lie."

He moved easily to his cluttered desk, leaned his hips against it, and folded his arms. "The hell you say! After all, I've known you only a few days. You're assuming a lot to come here and . . ."

"You've known Maureen longer."

"A couple of weeks. Not very long."

"You're repeating yourself," I said. "Repeating another little lie. You say you met her two weeks ago—after the death of Alec Martin's wife and child."

"I didn't know Maureen had killed a couple of people."

"She's not here to contradict you."

"That's right."

"She was a discreet woman. She valued her marriage and reputation. She wanted you to meet me—and when she introduced you to our crowd it would be in my company, as my friend as well as hers."

He shrugged. His face was composed, but his eyes were evasive. "You got anybody to prove I knew her before the death of the Martin woman and kid?"

"I sure as hell have. Maureen proved it herself. Unwittingly, she left proof to explode your defense."

"Yeah?"

"A month ago—before the death of Martin's wife and child—Maureen wrote to an agent about your work and sent him a couple of plays."

The color began to leave his face. "She shouldn't have done that! Not until I was ready, had something really great . . ."

"She liked surprises, Randy. She liked trying to help people. It would have given her a lot of satisfaction if she could have told you one of your plays had sold."

"Now look, Steve," he said. "Let's not make a mountain out of a molehill. Maybe I did meet her more than two weeks ago. You know how one talks: 'a couple of weeks ago'—just in the sense of an event happening some time ago."

"It doesn't ring true, Price. You didn't want to be connected with her at any time before Martin's wife and child were killed. You didn't want that connection because you knew about the accident. And if you knew, you were there when it happened!"

His face was gray.

"The Martin woman and child were killed early in the evening," I said. "The police have the exact time. Right after dinnertime. You were coming from dinner, weren't you, from one of the new places just beyond the city limits? You were returning to the city and cutting across West End on your way to Meade Park.

"There are certain kinds of restaurants Maureen favored. If I wanted to waste the time, I could take you to them. You—and a picture of Maureen. They're not limitless in number. Both of you would be easily remembered, she with her looks and you with that Vandyke on the boy face."

"What do you mean, 'waste the time'?"

"I'm certain you're the man. It happened just as I said.

142

Knowing where to look, the police could pin down every detail. But the police aren't here, are they, Randy?"

"Steve—"

"Her blood was all over the scum of Timmons Street. But when I got there, there were only chalk marks, an outline of the shell of my wife!"

He looked away, then back at my eyes. He slid along the desk, backing away, around it. A precariously balanced stack of magazines spilled to the floor.

"They'll get you, Steve—the way Martin caught up with her and the way you've caught up with me." He was shaking.

I said, grimly, "You have just enough time to tell me all of it."

"You can't do this to me Steve! You can't do it! Remember what you said about decency! You're decent too. Your decency won't let you do it!"

"It's my decency that tells me to do it!"

Tears came to his eyes. It wasn't an act this time, such as he'd put on when Reynolds and I had come here as strangers. He stood there weeping in a desperation of self-pity and frustration. "She treated me like a kid," he said. "Like a kid brother. That night—after dinner—she was lecturing me. She said I was young. Don't rush yourself, she said. Get a part-time job. Take time writing your plays. I laughed at her. As she turned into West End, she looked at me. And all of a sudden, there they were in the middle of the street, that woman and kid.

"Maureen didn't have time to stop. It was Alec Martin's wife's fault, Steve—not mine or Maureen's. The woman was looking at her husband, waving at him. When she jumped, she jumped the wrong way.

"There wasn't much sound, only the thud of something soft and yielding hitting the car. You expect something different when two people died.

"Maureen took her foot off the gas. She was going to stop. But I wouldn't let her. I was crazy with panic. All I wanted to do was get away from there. The car had skidded when Maureen tried to miss the woman and kid. She was fighting it to a stop. I grabbed her and told her to get the hell out of there! She was so scared she couldn't speak, but she looked at me and shook her head. I grabbed the steering wheel, kicked her foot off the brake, and stepped on the gas. I had my body half across her, holding her against the seat." He paused, looking at me for understanding. What he saw in my face caused his to go even grayer.

"You forced her to drive on," I said.

"You can see it wasn't our fault, Steve!" he cried.

"What did you do next?"

He licked his lips. "I brought the car here and cleaned up the front end. Maureen sat on the porch steps and cried. She was shaking all over. I tried to calm her. She kept saying we had to go back. She made me leave the car radio on, and during a newscast we heard that the woman and child were dead, but that the car hadn't been identified.

"I knew we could never go back. I tried to make her see that. They'd have us for manslaughter now, for running away. And my work"—his voice broke—"my whole future, everything, would be destroyed, because of a stupid woman and child. I could never live in prison. If they shut me up, I'd die. My genius would waste away and be lost to the world forever. I was young. I hadn't even started yet. All my years, my freedom, the plays to be written were before me. I couldn't risk all that, could I? We couldn't help them by going back. Going back would see me in prison for manslaughter, with nothing gained for anybody. That's logical, Steve, isn't it? Isn't it, Steve?"

I understood only that his ego would never permit him to admit to being wrong, no matter what he did or how he did it. He would always be the poor, innocent victim of circumstance.

He was too precious to himself to do anything other than what he'd done. He saw the whole world, its people, its events in relation to the only thing that mattered to him—his ego.

"How did you keep Maureen from going back?" I asked.

"I tried to talk to her, to show her how senseless it would be. Then I told her that before I'd throw away my work, my future, all that I am—before I'd bury myself in prison—I'd do something desperate. I thought we were safe. I thought that as long as I worked continually on Maureen and she kept quiet we'd be all right. I thought that in time, after she had got used to living with the thing, she'd cease to be a danger to me. I never let her forget she'd foul up your life and Penny's—which meant more to her than her own life.

"The next day I stole a set of license plates and put them on the car. I took it to a grubby garage and had the fender and front headlight fixed. Then I put the proper plates back on the car and took it to her."

Everything was clear now. Here, in the presence of his monstrous ego, I could understand how he had taken the next step. Once Alec Martin showed up, Randy had to silence him. Any other decision would have been unthinkable. Any other course of action would have been impossible. What was the already shattered life of a faceless grocer in a cheap end of town worth when compared to Randy's freedom, future, and work? Nothing mattered to Randy Price except Randy Price. Not even Maureen, who had wanted to help him. When Martin went, she had to go too, because for him it was the only way out.

As if he sensed what was going on in my mind, he explained: "I'm not a criminal, Steve. None of it was my fault. I couldn't help it. It was forced on me . . ." One of his hands was on the desk before him, nervously wandering among his papers. Suddenly he moved. For a brief instant I glimpsed the heavy paperweight in his hand and tried to duck. My instinctive movement probably saved my life, for it struck my forehead a glancing blow, enough to lay open a good-sized gash. The force of it almost knocked me down. As I regained my footing, I heard the screen door slam.

He was moving down the driveway like a broken field runner when I got outside. But my car was parked behind his, and I was behind him with the gun. He glanced back, saw me, ducked, and changed direction, moving across the level of empty field that stretched east of the cottage. Beyond was timber, safety. He knew he had a chance, a swift, darting target extremely hard to hit with a revolver. It would take something bigger than a bullet from a small pistol to hit him and something a lot faster than I to catch him.

Something like a big dark green sedan.

21

He'd reached the middle of the field when he heard the surging roar of the car coming up behind him. He looked over his shoulder and saw the sedan, the same kind of car that had killed Maureen and carried Martin to the bottom of the river.

He leaped to one side, and the car veered past.

I twisted the wheel. The car slued around and moved toward him again like an enraged bull.

He was running in the other direction now, back toward the cottage. Again he heard the car and looked over his shoulder. Through the windshield I could see his white face slick with sweat. I could see the round black hole of his mouth laboring for breath. He timed the car by the sound of the motor and threw himself to one side at the final instant.

He was off in a third direction, away from the street, angling toward the timber. He began to wobble as his long legs broke stride.

He tripped.

He didn't have the reserve to get up. He quit cold, huddled on his knees, hands covering his face, waiting for the car.

I slammed on the brakes, inches away, got out, and walked

toward him. I stood over him, watching the violent shaking of his body as he looked up at me.

"You're—not going to—"

"No," I said wearily. "I thought I could, but I can't." I stirred him with the toe of my shoe. "Get up," I said. "We're going back to town—to Headquarters." He fell face forward on the clean earth and lay there with his stomach convulsing.

I looked at the horizon. The light, I saw, of the setting sun had changed. The blood red had drained from the west, and cool twilight had begun to settle on the field, bringing a promise of peace.

Perhaps at this very instant Vicky and Penny were dining with great ceremony, on a little lake bream caught with a bent pin and a piece of string. . . .